The Social Emergency
Studies in Sex Hygiene and Morals

Various

Contents

THE SOCIAL EMERGENCY

STUDIES IN SEX HYGIENE AND MORALS

BY

Various

PREFACE

This volume is the outgrowth of an extension course conducted by Reed College in Portland, Oregon, in 1913. The course was offered to teachers and to workers in various other fields of social service as an outline of the main problems of social hygiene and morals and as a guide to further study. An edition of forty-five hundred copies of the syllabus of the course was soon exhausted, and there appeared to be a sufficient demand for the publication of some of the lectures.

The chapters are the various lectures, condensed by the editor, but otherwise substantially as given, with the exception of chapters I, II, and XII, which are here presented for the first time. In the original course, Reed College fortunately had the services of Calvin S. White, M.D., and L.R. Alderman, officers of the Oregon Social Hygiene Society. Their addresses have been omitted, because they were prepared rather to meet local conditions and the needs of the course than for the general public. For the same reason the greater part of the addresses of William House, M.D., and of the editor have been omitted.

The Social Emergency does not purport to be a comprehensive or systematic treatment of the problems of sex hygiene and morals; it presents merely the views of a number of persons on certain phases of the subject. Although no writer is responsible for the ideas of any other writer, yet nearly all the writers have read and approved all the chapters. Furthermore, the editor has had the aid of other competent critics. The proof has been read by Maurice Bigelow, Ph.D., Professor of Biology, Teachers College, Columbia University; by Calvin S. White, M.D., Secretary of the State Board of Health of Oregon and President of the Oregon Social Hygiene Society; and by William Snow, M.D., Secretary of the American Social Hygiene Association. Others, including Edward L. Keyes, Jr., M.D., and Harry Beal Torrey, Ph.D., have read the particular chapters concerning which they could give expert opinion. The editor is grateful to all these men, and to Florence Read, Secretary of Reed Extension Courses, who has given valuable aid. With their help he has endeavored to avoid the errors, the exaggerations, the narrowness of view, and the hysteria that characterize some of the current discussions concerning sex and the social evil.

If there is one dominant truth in this volume, it is that any plan for meeting the social emergency that would relax the control of moral and spiritual law over sex impulses is antagonistic, not only to physical health, but as well to the highest development of personality and to the progressive evolution of human society.

W.T.F.

REED COLLEGE,
PORTLAND, OREGON,
April, 1914.

THE SOCIAL EMERGENCY

INTRODUCTION

By Charles W. Eliot

This book is a collection of essays by several authors on the various aspects of social hygiene, and on the proper means of forming an enlightened public opinion concerning the measures which society can now, at last, wisely undertake against the vices and evils which in the human race accompany bodily self-indulgence and lack of moral stamina.

Till within five years, it was the custom in families, churches, and schools, to say nothing about sex relations, normal or abnormal; and in society at large to do nothing about the ancient evil of prostitution, to provide neither isolation nor treatment for the worst of contagious diseases, and to regard the blindness, feeble-mindedness, sterility, paralysis, and insanity which result from those diseases as afflictions which could not be prevented. The progress of medicine within twenty years, both preventive and curative, has greatly changed the ethical as well as the physical situation. The policy of silence and concealment concerning evils which are now known to be preventable is no longer justifiable. The thinking public can now learn what these evils are, how destructive they are, and by what measures they may be cured or prevented. With this knowledge goes the responsibility and duty of applying it in defense of society and civilization.

This book is a sincere effort, first, to supply the needed knowledge of terrible wrongs and destructions; and, secondly, to indicate cautiously and tentatively the most available means of attacking the evils described. It is an attempt to enlighten public opinion on one of the gravest of modern problems--indeed, the very gravest, with the exception of the warfare between capital and labor. The book is not intended for children, or even for adolescents, but rather for parents, teachers, and ministers who have to answer the questions of children and youth about sex relations, or deal sympathetically with the victims of sexual vice.

All efforts to deal directly with sex relations in schools, churches, and clubs are hampered, and must be for some years to come, by the lack of competent instructors in that difficult subject. So far as instruction in educational institutions is concerned, it seems as if the normal schools and the colleges for men or for women must be selected for the first experiments on class instruction. Family instruction is in most cases impossible; because neither father nor mother is competent to teach the children what needs to be taught about both the normal and the disordered sex relations. The ministers and priests are as a rule equally incompetent. They can give precepts or orders, but not explanations or reasons. Considerate managers of large industries ought to have a keen interest in all social hygiene problems, because they nearly concern industrial efficiency; but it is only lately that business men have begun to understand the close connection between public health and industrial prosperity, and most of them are not well informed on the subject.

Against prostitution and drunkenness governments of many sorts have been struggling ineffectually for centuries. These two evils go together; but whether taken separately or together no government has yet adopted an effective mode of dealing with them. Fortunately medical science has lately placed in the hands of government, and of private associations, effective means of defense against the social vices and their consequences; and the new social ethics call loudly on all men of good will to enlist in the warfare against these ancient evils, which to-day are more destructive than ever before, because of the prevailing industrial and social freedom, and the new facilities for individual traveling, and the migration of masses of men.

This book is intended to arouse public sentiment, spread accurate knowledge, check rash enthusiasm, and promote well-informed and resolute action.

CHAPTER I

THE SOCIAL EMERGENCY

By William Trufant Foster

Concerning matters of sex and reproduction there has been for many generations a conspiracy of silence. The silence is now broken. Whatever may be the wisdom or the folly of this change of attitude, it is a fact; and it constitutes a social emergency.

Throughout the nineteenth century the taboo prevailed. Certain subjects were rarely mentioned in public, and then only in euphemistic terms. The home, the church, the school; and the press joined in the conspiracy. Supposedly, they were keeping the young in a blessed state of innocence. As a matter of fact, other agencies were busy disseminating falsehoods. Most of our boys and girls, having no opportunity to hear sex and marriage and motherhood discussed with reverence, heard these matters discussed with vulgarity. While those interested in the welfare of the young withheld the truth, those who could profit by their downfall poisoned their minds with error and half-truths. An abundance of distressing evidence showed that nearly all children gained information concerning sex and reproduction from foul sources,--from misinformed playmates, degenerates, obscene pictures, booklets, and advertisements of quack doctors. At the same time the social evil and its train of tragic consequences showed no abatement. The policy of silence, after many generations of trial, proved a failure.

The past few years have seen a sudden change. Subjects formerly tabooed are now thrust before the public. The plain-spoken publications of social hygiene societies are distributed by hundreds of thousands. Public exhibits, setting forth the horrors of venereal diseases, are sent from place to place. Motion-picture films portray white slavers, prostitutes, and restricted districts, and show exactly how an innocent girl may be seduced, betrayed, and sold. The stage finds it profitable to offer problem plays concerned with illicit love, with prostitution, and even with the results of venereal contagion. Newspapers that formerly made only brief references to corespondents, houses of bad repute, statutory offenses, and serious charges, now fill columns with detailed accounts of divorce trials, traffic in women, earnings of prostitutes, and raids on houses. Novels that might have been condemned and suppressed a few decades ago are now listed among "the best sellers." Lectures on sex hygiene and morals are given widely, over four hundred such lectures having been given under the auspices of a single society. Fake doctors, while obeying the letter of new laws, are bolder than ever in some directions and use the alarm caused by the production of **Damaged Goods**, for example, as a means of snaring new victims. Generations of silence, enforced by the powerful influence of social custom, have been suddenly followed by a campaign of pitiless publicity, sanctioned by eminent men and women, and carried forward by the agencies of public education that daily reach the largest number of human beings--namely, the press, the motion picture, and the stage.

This far-reaching change in the customs of society is fraught with immediate dangers, because we do not know whether the mere knowledge of facts concerning sexual processes, vices, and diseases will do a given individual harm or good. The effect of such information upon any person is unquestionably determined by his physiological age, by his nervous system, by the manner and time of the presentation of the subject; above all, by his will power and the controlling ideals that are acquired along with scientific facts. As yet, we have not discovered thoroughly trustworthy pedagogical principles, administrative methods, and printed materials for public education in matters of sex. So difficult and complicated are the problems, and so disastrous are mistakes in this field of instruction, that the home, the church, and the school--the institutions to which young people should naturally look for truth in all matters, the agencies best qualified to solve the problems--are extremely cautious and conservative. While these agencies, which are concerned primarily with the welfare of the individual, the family, and society, have made some efforts to solve the problems, and to discover a safe and gradual transition from the old order to the new, other agencies, concerned primarily with making money, have rushed in to exploit the new freedom and the universal interest in matters of sex. This passing of the old order, and the invasion of the new order before we are prepared for it, constitute the social emergency of the twentieth century. Great as are the industrial and political revolutions of modern times, it is doubtful if anything so deeply concerns the coming generations as our measure of success in confronting the present social emergency.

In no other phase of social education are mistakes so serious. Other changes, demanded by new ideas of the function of the school, have been made prematurely and clumsily, but without grave danger. We have adjusted ourselves readily enough to compulsory education, normal schools, higher education for women, expert supervision, the kindergartens, physical training, industrial schools, university extension, care of defectives, and vocational guidance. Every new type of school and every new subject has been introduced before there were teachers trained for the new work. We stumbled along. Few were greatly concerned over mistakes in the teaching of penmanship and spelling and millinery and Latin and algebra. Few protested against the inefficient teaching of physiology as long as it rattled only dry bones, and had no evident relation to the physical functions and health of the student. But the moment men proposed to teach a subject of vital consequence, there was a cry of protest--and rightly.

Here mistakes will not do: here incompetent teachers cannot be trusted. Ill-advised efforts to teach sex hygiene may aggravate the very evils we are trying to assuage. Because the subject is of vital importance, education in sexual hygiene and morals must proceed cautiously and conservatively; according to tried methods, psychologically sound; always under the control of men and women of maturity, who see the present emergency in its many phases, who know how to teach, whose character is in keeping with the highest ideals of their work, and who approach their subject with reverence and their pupils with the joy and inspiration which come from a large opportunity to serve mankind.

Unhappily, not all of those who have been stimulated by the new freedom of speech to thrust themselves forward as teachers of sex hygiene, and as social reformers, are safe leaders. Some are ignorant and unaware that enthusiasm is not a satisfactory substitute for knowledge. Some are hysterical. At a recent purity convention, a woman said, "I know little about the facts, but it is wonderful how much ignorance can accomplish when accompanied by devotion and persistence." That declaration was applauded. Some people appear to believe that they will arrive safely if they go rapidly enough and far enough, even though they may be going in the wrong direction. Many retard the movement for social hygiene by making statements they do not know to be true, especially in respect to the extent of sexual immorality, the number of prostitutes, and the prevalence of venereal disease. Young people of opposite sexes, finding evidence on every hand that the traditional taboo is removed, discuss the subject for personal pleasure.

The books in the field of social hygiene which have most scrupulously and successfully avoided everything that might be sexually stimulating are not the ones bought by the largest numbers. The demand for erotic publications is so great as to warn us in advance that the new freedom will prove dangerous for many whose minds are already unclean. The propaganda for social purity is unlike many others, in that there is special danger of doing injury to the very ones in special need of help. The fact that the young, the ignorant, the hysterical, and the sexually abnormal, as well as commercialized agencies, are using the newfound license in dangerous ways is reason enough for the liberal and whole-hearted support of the American Social Hygiene Association and affiliated societies.

These private organizations are striving to meet the present social emergency. They are temporary expedients. Their chief aim is public education. They should frustrate the efforts of all dangerous agencies and hasten the day when the home, the church, and the school shall meet their full responsibilities in the teaching of sexual hygiene and morals.

CHAPTER II

VARIOUS PHASES OF THE QUESTION

By William Trufant Foster

It is necessary to take into account all phases of the social emergency. The question is not merely one of physiology, or pathology, or diseases, or wages, or industrial education, or recreation, or knowledge, or commercial organization, or legal regulation, or lust, or social customs, or cultivation of will power, or religion. It is all of this and more. The danger is that we shall see only one or two sides of a many-sided problem. A solution may appear adequate because it leaves essential factors out of consideration.

One physiological factor in the situation is of fundamental importance, namely, the discrepancy between the age of sexual maturity and the prevailing age of marriage,--an artificial condition largely determined by social customs, by modern educational systems, and by standards of living. While society has set forward, generation after generation, the age at which marriage seems feasible, the age of puberty has remained virtually the same. This unnatural condition--as artificial as the clothes we wear--is a phase of the emergency which should be considered by those who condemn as unnatural and forced the education of adolescent boys and girls in sexual hygiene and morals. Partly as a result of this has come the general acceptance of the double standard of chastity which has bitterly condemned the girl--made her an outcast of society--and excused the boy for the same offense, on the false plea of physiological necessity.

With the sanction of this double standard, tacitly accepted by society, thousands of prostitutes have been harbored and protected. What shall we do with them? We may drive them out of certain districts and certain houses, and even certain cities, but they are still with us, and we are responsible for them. If they are denied resorts where men seek them, they will seek men. Most of them are unable, without special training, to earn a living in any other way, and many of them would not if they could. A majority are mentally defective and should be wards of society. Any plan which fails to take care of these women--adequately, permanently, and humanely--ignores one of the greatest of the problems which history, with the sanction of society, has made a factor of the present emergency.

The medical phase of the present situation is not often ignored, except by those who hold that there is no such thing as disease. All countries are alarmed over the prevalence of venereal infection. Definite information, however, concerning the extent of these diseases, the sources and conditions of contagion, and the complications and results, is not to be had; because society still persists in treating venereal diseases as not subject to public registration and control, in spite of their terrible attacks on tens of thousands of innocent victims.

The fear of contracting disease has long been used in attempts to promote a single standard of chastity. Such fear has no doubt played its part and will continue to keep many prudent men away from prostitutes. But in looking forward to the work of the next generation, we must face the need of higher motives than the fear of disease, for science may at any time discover positive safeguards against contagion, thus diminishing one of the factors of the present emergency and by the same stroke accentuating others.

Of the economic phases of the emergency, there are some which directly affect the wage-earner. One is the failure of wages to keep pace with the higher cost of living; another is the increase in the number and proportion of wage-earning women and the resultant keenness of competition for places; another is the fact that women workers are for the most part unorganized and unprotected; another is the occasional effect of supplementary wages of vice in lowering the wages of women in industry; still another is the constant temptation of shop-girls to imitate their patrons' vulgar displays of finery. But of all the economic factors contributing to the moral breakdown of girls, the most general and inexcusable is the failure of our public schools to provide vocational training, although it is certain that above fifty per cent of all girls leave the schools to become wage-earners. Failure to gain a living wage is undoubtedly one of the causes, though seldom the sole cause, of the first delinquency of some girls.

Other economic conditions serve to promote and intrench the business of prostitution. These conditions are as real as any other factors and will block reform until they are squarely met. One of these is the excessive profit on property used for immoral purposes. The fact that such property is often owned by persons who pass as respectable members of society does not make the problem easier. Then there is the intimate connection between the sale of intoxicating liquors and commercialized prostitution, as definitely revealed by the investigations of every vice commission.

Another economic factor intrenching prostitution as a business is the commercial organization which continues to do an international and interstate business, partly because of our inadequate white-slave laws and inadequate appropriation for enforcement.

Most important among the economic aids to prostitution as a business are the high immediate wages of vice in contrast with the low wages of virtue. A girl in the shop, or factory, or office may be capitalized at six thousand dollars; in the clutches of a procurer, she may become worth twenty-six thousand dollars. As a prostitute, she "earns more than four times as much as she is worth as a factor in the social and industrial economy, where brains, intelligence, virtue and womanly charm should bring a premium." In an average lifetime, to be sure, the wages of one woman in industry are greater than the earnings in the short life of one prostitute; but from the viewpoint of the man who pockets most of the earnings, it is more profitable to kill off a dozen women than to keep one at decent work through an average lifetime. This economic condition is revealed to the cast-out woman after a few years, on the brink of the grave; but at the outset of her brief career, she sees the immediate gain, not the ultimate ruin.

There are other economic factors which will aid all movements for social hygiene when they are more clearly perceived by those engaged in reputable business: first, the loss to honest industry due to the reduced efficiency of sexual perverts, of the diseased, and of those who, through their ignorance, have been kept in worry by "leading specialists"; and, in the second place, the inevitable reduction in the profits of legitimate business due to the excessive profits of illegitimate business.

The recreational pursuits of young people are other factors of immediate concern to those who would see the problems of social hygiene in their entirety. Adolescent boys and girls spend most of their leisure time either in wholesome physical activity conducive to normal sex life or in various forms of amusement fraught with danger. In seeking innocent recreation, young people can hardly escape contact with amusements cunningly devised to excite sex impulses and at the same time to lower respect for woman. The bill-boards and the picture post-cards, the penny-in-the-slot machines and the motion pictures, the exhibits of quack doctors, vaudeville performances, many so-called comic operas, popular new songs, the dress of women approved by modern fashion,--these all help at times to prepare young people to fall before the special temptations that beset all commercial recreation centers. Especially dangerous are the saloons, billiard rooms, dance-halls, ice-cream parlors, road-houses and amusement parks. Both male and female enemies of decency frequent these resorts. They are often schools of sexual immorality, with clever and persistent teachers. Unless we take them into due account, we cannot see the whole problem of education in sexual hygiene and morals.

Then there are the legal phases of the situation. We must consider, on the one hand how much can be accomplished by legislation, in view of all the known factors in the situation. Our courts, for example, in spasmodically or regularly rounding up women, fining them ten or fifteen dollars apiece, and turning them loose, are trying to meet the social emergency by shutting their eyes to nine out of ten of its essential features. Their policy gives a clean bill to the male prostitute, arrests the woman, takes away a part of her earnings, sets her free under the necessity of seeking new victims to offset the fine, offers her no incentive to lead any other life, incidentally increases opportunities for police graft, and virtually gives the sanction of the law to the whole nefarious business. The ostrich with his head buried in the sand sees our gravest social problem about as clearly and wholly as do many who are administering laws concerning prostitution in American cities.

The impotence of laws passed in advance of public education and public demand is a difficulty often overlooked. Some reformers seem to think they can eliminate the social evil by getting a law passed. They urge state legislatures to pass laws requiring every school to teach sex hygiene. These people think they are going straight at a solution; but they fail to see the patent fact that there are not now enough competent teachers for this work; no, not one teacher for every hundred schools. Another example of futile legislation is the California law requiring the reporting of cases of venereal diseases. One could easily list a score of laws in the domain of sexual morals which are ineffective, either because in their very nature they could not be enforced, or because the public do not wish to have them enforced. Perhaps there are no factors of the social emergency so frequently left out of account as the relation of public education to public opinion and the relation of public opinion to the possibility of law enforcement.

As a matter of fact the educational phases of social reform are of most immediate importance. Nothing can so profitably occupy the attention of social hygiene societies as the education of the public. If groups of social workers come to serious disagreement on other phases of the present emergency,--if the discussion of restricted districts, minimum-wage laws, health certificates for marriage, and reporting of diseases divides the group into warring camps,--all can unite in favor of spreading certain truths as widely as possible; and it is not difficult to agree on at least a few of the many methods which have already proved effective in educational campaigns.

At the outset of our attempt to educate the general public in matters of sex, we face certain factors which govern the scope, time, place, and method of any successful efforts. Failure to give these factors due consideration has brought many attempts to early and unhappy ends, and convinced some people that ignorance is safer than such education.

We must reckon carefully with the centuries of social tradition which have resulted in the taboo on the subjects of sex and reproduction. It may be that this conspiracy of silence has proved a failure; it may be that it has no basis worthy of intellectual respect. It may be that all people should welcome the new freedom of speech. These are not issues in the process of education. Our first concern is the actual state of the public mind; we begin with that or else we fail.

Biologically the all-inclusive issue concerns the survival of the race. Nature has no favorites: the fittest of the human stock will survive after others have degenerated and disappeared; the fittest animals will ultimately people the earth. Sexual degeneracy is the surest road to race extinction.

No aspects are more important than those concerning morals and religion. The restraining influences of the fear of disease may and probably will be thrown off by science. Whether education in scientific aspects of the subject will do good or harm in a given case depends on the extent to which moral and religious ideals control the conduct of the individual. The inadequacy of mere knowledge in the realm of sex hygiene is painfully evident. To the knowledge of what is right must be added the will to do the right. As moral and religious instruction is the dominant educational need of the present generation, so the moral and religious aspects of sex problems transcend all others in importance.

These are the most important phases of the social emergency. It is difficult to see them in all their intricate relationships and to realize that in any one approach we touch only one side of a many-sided problem. The great majority of our people see only the superficial aspects, or see one particular phase in distorted perspective, because that is brought close to them through a special case of misfortune. Even social workers are in danger of narrowness of vision because of devoted service in particular fields. The aim of the following chapters is to consider successively and in right relationships various aspects of the social emergency.

CHAPTER III

PHYSIOLOGICAL ASPECTS

By William House

All instruction in the physiology of reproduction as an aid to sexual hygiene should be so conducted as to give assurance that the wonders of the origin and development of life in all its millions of forms be taught in a respectful, even reverent, spirit. Naught in the universe is more marvelous than the beginnings of life. Naught else compares with the wonders of growth and development.

Rightly taught, reproduction may be cleansed from the foul interpretations which have soiled the minds of countless children, and may be made into a body of wonderful and sacred truths capable of fortifying youthful minds against the uncleanness and indecencies which have contributed so largely to sexual impurity. If it be never forgotten that human ingenuity has been taxed in untold numbers of unsuccessful experiments to produce life by other than nature's methods, while the power of reproduction resides in even the lowliest of living organisms, the mystery and marvel are multiplied a hundredfold, and the subject of reproduction is invested with a halo of splendid and inspiring proportions.

* * * * *

The sex organs are the agencies by which every plant and every animal, each after its kind, brings into the world a succeeding generation. Sex activity is the result of sex impulse. The imperative need of reproduction in the scheme of nature is responsible for the presence of sex impulse as it occurs in every normal adult animal. Were it not for this impulse the earth would soon become void of life. The human sex impulse is a powerful one, thought compelling, at times well-nigh overmastering. Though in the main good, it sometimes produces harmful results. Among the lower animals the sex function is exercised without thought or knowledge of consequence, restrained only by the limitations of physical power,--the power to obtain by might, by conquest. In fully developed mankind, the mind acts as a constraining force which may control or even completely subdue physical manifestations of sex impulse.

In adolescents--those who are approaching *maturity*, but are in a transition state, neither man nor child--sex desire may be as strong as in those of riper years. Many who are passing through this period know little or nothing of the forces that pulse through their frames and seem to consume them with unquenchable fires. These forces are the sex impulses, the beginning of sex life and sex activity. And as every work of man or nature while in a state of transition is unstable, less firmly founded, more easily destroyed or injured than at any other time, so it is that the adolescent finds himself in greater danger than at any other time of life. Consumed with incomprehensible desire, which he cannot gratify, he is the victim of circumstances which cause him distress, yet admit of no relief.

Probably all marriage laws have as their real object the protection of child life. Without marriage laws there could be no organized society and the human race would soon sink to the level of the animal world in general. Under present social conditions marriages are put off longer and longer. Each succeeding generation is marked by an increase in the age of those who marry. But the conditions which cause late marriages in no way lessen the sex impulses or mitigate the distress which these impulses cause. The impulse to multiply is neither greater nor less than in the past when marriages generally occurred earlier. Fortunately it is weaker in the female than in the male. There are those who believe that the male must exercise it if he would achieve his full strength of mind and body. Certain political and philosophic sects take cognizance of this belief and advocate legalized provision for the gratification of the sex impulse even to the extent of providing for the destruction of the lives of the unborn.

The most pernicious of the false beliefs regarding physiological necessity are as follows:--

1. That a life of sexual continence is not consistent with the best physical health.

2. That the exercise of the sex function is necessary to the full development and preservation of "manly power,"--the power of procreation.

3. That the sexual impulse in man is so imperious that it is impossible to control it and, therefore, a sexually continent life cannot be expected of man.

4. That, therefore, the moral standard which we apply to woman cannot be applied to man.

To correct these erroneous beliefs about the sex function, Dr. M.J. Exner brought together the testimony of the foremost medical authorities of the United States. He drew up a statement regarding sexual continence, and submitted it to leading physiologists for criticism so as to bring its phraseology wholly within the requirements of scientific precision. It was then submitted for endorsement to leading medical authorities throughout the country. The ready and hearty response of 370 of these men in endorsing the declaration leaves no doubt as to the conviction of the leading men of the medical profession on this question. The declaration is as follows:--

"In view of the individual and social dangers which spring from the widespread belief that continence may be detrimental to health, and of the fact that municipal toleration of prostitution is sometimes defended on the ground that sexual indulgence is necessary, we, the undersigned, members of the medical profession, testify to our belief that continence has not been shown to be detrimental to health or virility; that there is no evidence of its being inconsistent with the highest physical, mental and moral efficiency; and that it offers the only sure reliance for sexual health outside of marriage."[1]

The erroneous beliefs concerning physiological necessity have been propagated chiefly on the authority of advertising medical fakers, whose business depends on misrepresentation and deceit, men whose methods exclude them from the ranks of reputable physicians. They are also taught by those within the ranks of the profession who are ignorant or unscrupulous or both, and who for the most part have no higher incentive in their profession than the pursuit of the dollar. The teaching of these men is in most cases more an expression of their own vicious habits than of real conviction. Both wholly misrepresent the teaching and attitude of the great majority of physicians who constitute the reputable body of the profession.

Dr. William H. Howell, Professor of Physiology at Johns Hopkins University, says: "There is no evidence whatsoever that the sexual appetite or the act of reproduction has any physiological relationship to the preservation of the integrity of the individual. This appetite has been created or evolved and made strong in us for an entirely different purpose. A sexual necessity exists only so far as the integrity of the race is concerned; so far as the individual is concerned his sexual functions may be unused or he may be completely unsexed without any injury to his bodily health."

NOTES:

[1] The full list of authorities is given in ***The Physician's Answer***, by

M.J. Exner, M.D., Secretary, Student Department, International Committee,

Young Men's Christian Associations, Association Press, New York, 1913.

This is the best treatment of the question of physiological necessity. It

is freely quoted in this chapter. [Editor.]

CHAPTER IV

MEDICAL PHASES

By Andrew C. Smith

Some idea of the prevalence of venereal diseases in the United States may be obtained from the following statistics of the census for 1910. The registration area covered a population of 48,877,893 persons. The figures are here extended to cover a population of 90,000,000 people: Deaths ascribed to venereal disease, 5275; spinal cord diseases, 2598; paresis, 4845. Other diseases partly due to syphilis: softening of the brain, a term indiscriminately used to cover a number of diseases including brain syphilis and paresis, 2111; paralysis, usually meaning apoplexy, but always including many cases of brain syphilis, 14,479; premature birth, by some believed to be the result of syphilis in one half of all cases, 34,174; congenital debility, deaths due in many cases to feebleness of the child resulting from syphilis, 25,285; blindness, one fourth the total number of blind in this country estimated at 15,000 to 20,000. Many estimate that over half of the entire male population have had gonorrhea. The principal reason for this alarming distribution among all classes of these infections and their steady increase is ignorance and misunderstanding of physiological facts, particularly the viciously false teaching of the street corner that sexual activity is a physiological necessity.

These diseases would be arrested were there a widespread knowledge of their disastrous effects. Although young men hear the mischievous lie that "gonorrhea is no worse than a bad cold," thousands of them are punished with sterility as a result of the disease. Nearly all the neglected cases result in so-called ascending infections, reaching the bladder and kidneys and causing many deaths, and many men carry the infection in dormant form, to infect innocent wives in later years.

Appalling as are the consequences of gonorrheal infection in men, they are not so fatal or so far-reaching as syphilis. The causative parasite of this disease spares not a single tissue in the body and may disturb any or all of its functions, not even mentality escaping. As a cause of death it is extremely frequent. Our statistics ordinarily ascribe to syphilis but a small percentage of the deaths actually due to it; for instance, many of our cases of spinal disease, paralysis, arterial and other organic diseases are tabled under other names, although directly due to syphilis.

In women gonococcic infections are even more destructive than in men, as it is extremely common for the infection to extend to the tubes and to the peritoneal cavity, thus necessitating dangerous and mutilating operations, generally followed by sterility and often by death. Syphilis, though less frequent in women than in men, is nearly if not quite as fatal as in men, and otherwise similar in its baneful effects. I The child suffers the most tragic results of venereal infection, for it is always wholly innocent, yet infected to a greater or less extent, if the parents be syphilitic, and frequently if the birth-canal be gonorrheally infected. Although silver nitrate is a remedy for gonorrheal infection, if applied to the eyes immediately after birth, nevertheless the babe frequently suffers with infected eyes, and not infrequently with blindness.

If the child's sad infection is syphilis, instead of gonorrhea, there are still other miseries in store for it. If it is not so fortunate to be stillborn, it may have infection that ranges from almost imperceptible degrees to the most loathsome extent that it is possible for animal tissue to harbor. Its brain may be so invaded by the syphilitic parasites that it can never attain any degree of mentality; its spinal column maybe so involved that paralytic conditions will surely result; and if these nerve centers escape special involvement, other organs may be affected, such as the stomach, bowels, and liver; if these escape, the bones may be so deficient in vitality as to be incapable of sustaining the frame as development proceeds; the skin only may be involved, or the mucous membranes so affected as to make of the child a perpetual snuffler and inefficient breather. In most cases of lesser as well as greater mental defect, the tests show syphilitic infection. Endless are the complications that may be visited upon the innocent progeny of syphilitic antecedents.

The gonorrheal infections occur in the mucous membranes lining the cavities, especially those of the urethra and female genital tract. It is in these tissues that the germ of gonorrhea finds lodgment, and once there its development is hard to interrupt. Although the growth of the gonorrheal germ produces acute symptoms, such as discharge and pain, these pass off under treatment in a few weeks. Unfortunately the disease is far from cured, for the microbe has found its natural habitat in the inter-cellular structure of the genital mucus, from which it cannot readily be dislodged, and from which it may invade other tissues. It may remain in a state of latency for an indefinite time; then transferred to a new field, it may resume its original activities. While in this stage of latency it is difficult to destroy. At this time it is more likely to be further disseminated, as the patient, ignorant of the condition, is more likely to convey the disease, which so often occurs in married life after a long forgotten infection.

The gonococcus (the microbe of gonorrhea) is a pus--producing bacterium, occurring in pairs, resembling in form two coffee grains, generally with a distinct interval of separation. Although its natural habitat is the mucous membrane lining the genito-urinary tracts it may invade the muscular and serous and other tissues. If often affects the Fallopian tubes and ovaries and the serous lining of the pelvic and abdominal cavities. The deeper sub-mucous tissues of the uterus and the male genito-urinary tracts are also frequently involved, it being sometimes impossible to eradicate it from these deeper retreats. From these deeper tissues it is more commonly taken up by the circulation and deposited in distant parts, frequently in the joints. When it becomes thus systematically disseminated, the so-called secondary or metastatic lesions are almost as numerous, though not as virulent, as syphilitic infection. Recent pathological researchers have found that occasionally the gonococcus becomes the causative factor in inflammations of the muscles, tendons, and glands, and in inflammatory conditions of the lungs, kidneys, heart, and even the brain, spinal cord, and the serous membranes enveloping these great cranial and spinal viscera.

The individuality and characteristics of the syphilis microbe were not positively determined until in 1905, Schaudinn, of Germany, convinced the medical world that it was a spiral, corkscrew-like organism, from a quarter to one millimeter in thickness, and from four to twelve millimeters in length. It is not so discriminating as the gonococcus in its points of inoculation, nor is it as vulnerable to attack; and it is vastly more destructive to the tissues invaded. It spares no tissue in the human frame, and resists destruction by any known drugs of vegetable origin. When in a latent state its presence was often impossible to determine until, two years after its discovery, a test was worked out by Wasserman, also of Germany, by which diagnosis of the infection may be made,--even in latent form,--as in a hereditary case where no clinical manifestations have yet asserted themselves. There is another valuable blood test worked out by Noguchi. With these two tests we are now able to diagnose the disease, almost absolutely, and follow up the treatment till cure is complete, except in some of the incurable brain and spinal cord cases.

In 1909, Ehrlich determined, after a series of laboratory experiments on animals inoculated with the syphilis germ (spirochaeta pallida), that a complex compound, with arsenic as its base, had the desired effect of destroying the parasite, in a dose not poisonous to the animal. This compound, first designated as "606," representing its number among his many laboratory experiments, he later named "salvarsan." With the assistance of his clinical friends, he soon demonstrated the action of his compound on man, and gave it freely to the world. Although it is now almost universally used, it has not proved to be the absolute cure that it was hoped it would be, as some of the spirochaetae seem to be hidden away where they are protected from the circulating poison,--to bring forth new progeny,--thus producing so-called recurrence.

The possibility of the infection of innocent persons is always uppermost in the mind of the medical man, and should equally concern the layman. Contaminated articles and utensils, such as towels and common drinking-cups, have caused many infections. This danger is greater from syphilis than from gonorrhea, for the reason that the spirochaeta pallida is more virulent than the gonococcus. In our own fields, camps, and mines, it is common for men to drink from one jug or dipper. Infection almost surely follows if one of the crowd has a syphilitic sore on the lip. So intense is the activity of the spirochaeta pallida in the primary stage that it may be borne to innocent parties by unwashed clothes and utensils of any kind, that have been in recent contact with a primary syphilitic sore. A dentist's or a doctor's instruments, for instance, are extremely dangerous as infection carriers, if they are not thoroughly sterilized by boiling. The danger of infection in syphilis and gonorrhea depends largely upon the virulence of the individual infection. As some living tubercle bacilli may be harbored and thrown off with impunity, while others will destroy the strongest man, regardless of all treatment, so some spirochaetae or gonococci may be safely disposed of, while others are most deadly.

Of all the sad instances of germ infection, the saddest are those from venereal germs, for they are disseminated mostly in vice, and inoculated into the innocent through ignorance. A common cause of infection of the innocent is the false popular belief that venereal germs are transmitted only in sexual congress. The truth is that any part of the body is in danger of inoculation from syphilis if the germ be virulent. So may any membranous point be infected by the gonococcus, whether conveyed by hand or instrument or fabric. This explains the number of gonococcic infections occurring in girl children. They come in membranous contact (at the outlet of vagina or rectum, or in the eye) with a contaminated article of clothing, or with the contaminated hands of an infected person. Ignorance is the cause of nearly all venereal infections. Why, then, should venereal infection not be eradicated? With adequate education, if there is not eradication, there will at least be compensation, for the sacrifice will be mainly of those who will not accept education--the unfit.

The possibility of recovery from syphilis is greater at present than it has been in the past, but we cannot yet say that the disease is absolutely curable in a given case. While most cases treated early with salvarsan, and followed by judicious use of mercury, are curable, there are nevertheless those which do not thus respond, and which in spite of all treatment go from bad to worse, till the patient's miseries are ended in insanity, paralysis, and death.

While the venereal diseases are the greatest physical evils to be attributed to sex ignorance, there are others chargeable to the same cause. There are, for instance, important physiological phenomena pertaining to sex development, ignorance of which is often baneful to the developing adolescent of either sex. When the boy's voice begins to change, and hair begins to appear on his face and body, and more thrilling sensations occasionally command his attention, he should be told, modestly but distinctly, that a pure and manly function is developing within him, the sole object of which is reproduction, and he must not consider it in a vulgar way, nor discuss it with others than his parents or physician or minister. Tell him that these physical changes of oncoming manhood are due to the establishment of the secretion of the procreative fluid,--the semen,--and will be safely cared for by nature. Fortify him against the mental pollution of the quack advertisement, and the satanically false teaching of ignorant associates that sexual intercourse is physiologically necessary, by impressing him with the fact that nature cares for the disposal of the seminal secretion. When clearly made aware of these simple sex principles, and convinced that it is unmanly and depraved to consider them vulgarly, the rapidly developing manly boy will not become a masturbator or a frequenter of bawdy-houses and a victim of the gonococcic or spirochaetic infections; nor will he become a moral assassin, a seducer of girls.

The sister, no less than the brother, needs pure, plain, non-prudish sex education. If her mother is not qualified to impart it, she, like the boy, should seek the aid of her minister, or physician, or a qualified school teacher; better a few suggestions from an experienced, modest source than many suggestions from inexperienced and often lewd companions. As the brother was told of the physical phenomena accompanying his sex development, so the sister should be apprised of the physiological necessity of her periodical functions, and of nature's kindly care and development of her delicate and wonderful sex mechanism, the sole purpose of which is maternity. It will fortify her maidenliness to tell her that much of the world is deceitful and degrading in sex matters, and that if she would be a perfect woman, mentally and physically, she must vigilantly guard her virtue, maintaining absolute purity, not only with persons of the opposite sex, but with persons of her own sex, and the person of her own self. Incalculable good can be done toward the uplift of wayward humanity by sex education.

CHAPTER V

ECONOMIC PHASES

By Arthur Evans Wood

In any effort for social improvement it is necessary to know conditions that make both for and against success. This is especially so in social hygiene, for it is closely related to all aspects of modern life. Lack of education and false instruction are largely responsible for sexual immorality. It is not so generally known that economic conditions are responsible for vice, opinions on this matter ranging all the way from a denial that economic conditions have anything to do with vice to the assertion that vice would disappear with the increase in the incomes of working-people. Assuming that ignorance is the fundamental cause of vice (an assumption which does not "stand to reason") the results of ignorance must manifest themselves through the institutions of society. Some institutions, such as slavery, encourage vice. Likewise, any caste system, such as feudalism in the Middle Ages, in which there must be depths as well as heights, supplies the vicious classes. The aim of this chapter is to show that, while modern economic conditions do not create "the social evil" they furnish an environment favorable to its spread. If this is so, an improvement in these conditions must accompany all other measures for the eradication of vice.

One of the most significant facts of the industrial evolution of the last half-century is the increase in the number of women who have become wage-earners outside the home. According to the Federal Census the number of females fifteen years of age and over, employed as breadwinners in 1900, was 5,007,069, an increase of 34.9 per cent over the number thus employed in 1890.[2] The largest number in any one occupation, 1,213,828, were servants and waitresses. Of this class the domestics were not employed "outside the home." The homes, however, were not their own, and salutary influences of home life do not exist for the majority of domestics. In the decade between 1900 and 1910 the increase in the number of wage-earning women has been even more accelerated than in previous decades, and to-day probably from 8,000,000 to 10,000,000 women in the United States are industrially employed.

One important aspect of this influx of women into industry is that the proportion of those in domestic and personal service, which has always been women's work, has decreased; whereas the proportion of those in manufacturing, trade, and transportation, which are new employments for women, has increased.[3] This means that not only are working-girls and women leaving the homes, but they are also abandoning in increasing numbers those occupations to which in times past their sex has been most accustomed. It is impossible that this prodigious change in the sphere and work of women should not be accompanied by some change in the social and moral standards that were nourished in the seclusion of the home. Miss Jane Addams has made the suggestion that perhaps the superior reputation of women for virtue is due to the fact that, generally speaking, women have been secluded from the influences of the world.[4]

The increase in the proportion of girls engaged in non-domestic pursuits means that industrial vocations for women are becoming more dissociated from the arts of home-making,--a fact which is doubtless the cause of many an inner struggle.

In the present lack of industrial education young girls who must work to support themselves or their families drift about from place to place with no definite vocational aims. Frequently they come to the offices of child labor commissions wanting work, but not knowing what they can do, or even what they would like to do. If they do find work, it is rarely of a sort that offers incentives for a career. Lack of skill, of interests, and of ambitions result in industrial inefficiency. They are also the usual accompaniments of moral delinquency.

Even where opportunities for industrial training are offered, they may not lessen the disparity between industrial opportunities that exist for girls and womanly tastes. A recent report on the need for a trade school for girls in Worcester, Massachusetts, advocates a school that will train for skill in the machine-operating trades, because there is most demand for workers in these trades.[5] One might think in reading the report that machines for stitching corsets and underwear provided the ideal vocation for women. Biological considerations, if no others, would favor distribution of wage-earning women away from the mechanical pursuits into those which are more or less associated with the domestic arts.

A further significance for social hygiene of the entrance of women into industry is that it places a strain upon the spirit of chivalry which is a basis of right relations between the sexes. Chivalry in men has accompanied the comparative seclusion of women from the world, and is due to those instincts which lead men to protect those who are weaker than themselves. The term "the weaker sex" has a sound physiological basis. With the passing of the domestic system of industry, however, the seclusion of women becomes more and more a thing of the past. In factory and shop they mingle promiscuously with men. Crowds of young working-girls in every large city at the noon hour throng the streets. If they walk to and from work they sometimes have to pass unprotected through parts of the city given over to vice.[6] They thus become familiar with vice conditions and are often subject to ungentlemanly, if not insulting, conduct. There are in every community a number of men who are decent only under restraint, and the economic position of wage-earning girls weakens that restraint.

Moreover, the phrase "the weaker sex" has lost some of its significance. Many occupations, such as clerking, stenographing, laundering, and certain kinds of unskilled factory work are almost entirely taken over by women, who labor throughout the same working-day as men, and usually at a lesser wage than men would receive for the same kind of work. Under these conditions, to talk of the physical weakness of women is to accuse our civilization of cruelty.

Around wages most of the discussion has centered concerning the economic aspect of vice. The investigations conducted throughout the country have revealed a great variety of opinion concerning the relation between low wages and immorality. There has been much confusion of thought on the question. It is true, on the one hand, that injustice is done to wage-earning girls and women of the country when the report is circulated that the difference between morality and immorality is only one of dollars and cents. On the other hand, to deny that low wages paid to working-girls has any bearing on the question of vice is evidence of failure to grasp the moral problem involved. Morality, to be sure, is always expressed in the overcoming of difficulties. Yet we can hold a person blameworthy only if in the full possession of his or her faculties. A poorly nourished, fatigued girl has no such self-possession. If she does not earn enough on which to live, and "goes wrong," her inadequate wage is a factor in her wrong-doing, and the one who pays it to her cannot be rid of his share of the responsibility. "Sin is misery, misery is poverty. The antidote for poverty is income,"[7] says Professor Simon N. Patten, who is doing a vast deal toward bringing economics and morals on speaking terms with each other.

Vice investigations in Chicago, Minneapolis, Portland, Oregon, Philadelphia, and elsewhere snow that there are many economic factors besides wages involved as causes of vice. Some of these other factors are housing, hours of work morally dangerous employments, associations at work, and fatigue. The wage, however, is more important than all of these, for the wage largely governs living conditions, associations and recreation. The wage often makes the difference between life as mere existence and life with the opportunities for self-improvement that should belong to a human being.

It will be of value, then, to note some of the facts about wages that have appeared in recent surveys made by the Consumers' League of Oregon, by the State of Massachusetts, and by the Federal Government. After showing that the minimum cost of living for a self-supporting woman in Portland is $10 a week, the Oregon Survey shows that in the nine principal occupations employing women in Portland, from 22 to 92 per cent are receiving less than $10 a week. The table is as follows:--

Occupations Per cent
      under $10

Department stores 58.2
Factories   74.7
Hotels and restaurants   49.2
Laundries   92.6
Offices (clerks)   46.4
Offices (stenographers)   22.4
Printing-shops   56.1
Telephone exchanges   50.

Miscellaneous   48.7

Another table shows that in five different employments,--laundries, factories, offices, department stores, and miscellaneous employment,--out of 509 women all but 31 (office workers) close the year with a deficit.[8]

A significant point is that among all but factory workers the excess of expenditures over incomes is greatest among those who live at home. This disproves the statement often made that those who live at home do not need a living wage. In conclusion, the *Report* of the Oregon Survey says: "The investigation has proved beyond a doubt that a large majority of self-supporting women in the State are earning less than it costs them to live decently; that many are receiving subsidiary help from their homes, which thus contribute to the profits of their employers; that those who do not receive help from relatives are breaking down in health from lack of proper nourishing food and comfortable lodging quarters, or are supplementing their wages by money received from immoral living."[9]

The Massachusetts Commission on Minimum Wage Boards reports even lower standards in wages for women. Among wage-earning girls and women over 18 years of age, 93 per cent of the candy-workers, 60 per cent of the workers in retail stores, and 75 per cent of laundry-women receive less than $8 a week.[10] In the cotton textile industry, among the 8021 women over 18 years of age whose wages were investigated, 38 per cent received less than $6 a week.[11] Among the individual stories that are buried in the *Report*, the following are typical:--

> Ernestine is an eighteen-year-old Canadian girl, very pretty and neatly dressed. Her parents both died several months ago and left her utterly alone, without living relatives. She worked as a stock girl at $4.50 a week for two months, was laid off, and went to a summer hotel as waitress for $3 a week, room and board. She worked there for two months, or until the season was over, and then came to another store

for $5 a week. She pays $1.50 for her room, including light and heat, has no carfare, does her laundering, except for shirt waists which cost her $.30 during the summer. She goes without breakfast or eats only a banana, gets her lunch for ten or fifteen cents, and her dinners for twenty or twenty-five cents. She has never paid more than twenty-five cents for a meal since she started to work. She is just a child, and is quite bewildered over the problem of facing life on $5 a week, and is terribly afraid of debt. She is intelligent and clever.[12]

Jennie is a frail little body, about 40 years old. After working 16 years in a Boston department store her wage was $5 a week.... For eleven years Jennie's little $5 a week had been the sole support of herself and her aged mother.... When her astonished employer learned that she had worked 16 years in his store and attained a wage of only $5 a week, he raised it $1. So the wage is supplemented by the girls (in the store) underpaid themselves, but comprehending the woman's need.... Thus seventeen years of faithful service to one master has won for Jennie this position of semi-dependence upon charity, increasing anxiety over an unprovided-for future, and declining health as a result of her pitiless struggle to stretch a miserable $5 over the cost of support of herself and mother.[13]

The most comprehensive report has been made by the Federal Government, and includes a survey of conditions among women in stores and factories in seven cities[14]. According to this report the average earnings of the women in retail stores of these cities is $6.88 in the case of those who live at home, and $7.89 in the case of those who are "adrift."[15] Among the factory women of these cities the average wage of those who live at home is $6.40, and of those who are "adrift," $6.78. The Boston investigation shows that from 11,000 to 12,000 women and girls were living in lodging- or boarding-houses at an average cost of $5.18 a week for prime necessities, leaving only $2.24 for clothing and all other expenses.

The following comment is made on this government report by the Massachusetts Minimum Wage Commission:--

> Although more than half the adrift women (in Boston) live in lodging- or boarding-houses,--numbering be it remembered between 11,000 and 12,000 girls and women,--two thirds of them lack the use of a sitting-room and must entertain men as well as women in their bedrooms. Not a few indications were seen in the course of the investigation of the demoralizing results of this practice. Many of the young women in lodgings were young and were friendless and were earning very low pay. Eighteen per cent of those who were reported without the use of a sitting-room were under twenty-five. The housing or food, or both, were reported as bad for a number of these perilously defenceless young women.[16]

Consideration of wages and standards of living leads to the question, What is a living wage? Studies in different parts of the country agree that it is about $10 a week. An estimate made by social workers for the Massachusetts Minimum Wage Commission places the minimum at $10.60 for girls who are adrift, and $8.37 to $8.71 for girls and women living at home. This estimate, however, made no allowance for unemployment, sickness, accident, or old age.[17] The Portland Vice Commission and the Consumers' League of Oregon have adopted a $10 minimum.[18] The first conference called by the Oregon Industrial Welfare Commission adopted $9.25 a week, or $40 per month, as "the sum required to maintain in frugal but decent conditions of living a self-supporting woman employed in mercantile establishments in Portland."[19] To this, however, representatives of the employees on the conference made objection, stating that a straight $10 a minimum was the only safe one.

If the minimum is rightly placed at $10, and if the investigations are true in showing that the majority of self-supporting women the country over are receiving less than this amount, we may now come to a more detailed discussion as to the relation between underpayment and vice. It is just here that it is easy to jump at conclusions. Most people approach social questions not with a scientific mind, but with preconceptions which mar their judgment. For example, the socialist exaggerates the effect of bad wage conditions, and the Woman's Auxiliary Department of the police exaggerate the influence of home conditions. Again, personal testimony is unreliable, because, on the one hand, victims of the social evil are liable to blame external conditions; and, on the other hand, well-fed, well-housed investigators often underestimate the bad moral effect of poor nourishment and fatigue.

Of this much we may be certain: low wages poor living, which involves poor housing, poor food, no savings, and either no recreation or dependence on others for it. In the federal report on living conditions of women in stores and factories, it is estimated that in the seven cities where the investigation took place approximately 65,000 women are adrift.[20] Since the majority of these are receiving less than the minimum cost of a decent living, they are "perilously defenseless young women."

Another federal report,[21] bearing directly on the relation between conditions of work and vice, concludes that whereas few girls "go wrong" on account of poverty, the misstep once taken, poverty and want are powerful deterrents to reform. A fourfold classification is made of immoral women, as follows: (1) Unmarried mothers; (2) girls who leave and regain the path of virtue, having their fling for the sake of good times; (3) occasional prostitutes, who enter the career as a business for a while; (4) professional prostitutes. Mention should be here made of this report, because its total effect is to minimize economic causes of prostitution, placing the responsibility elsewhere than on industrial conditions. It is to be noted, however, that it does emphasize the indirect effects of poverty, and does speak of the moral danger lurking in certain occupations, and of the bad effects of the lack of industrial education.

More definite responsibility for vice is ascribed to low wages in the reports of vice commissions. The Chicago *Report* says that of one group of 119 immoral women, 18 came from department stores, and 38 said that they had taken up the career for the need of money. The Portland *Report* presents 22 women as "Cases in which Low Wage and Vice are closely associated."[22] The *Report* continues:--

> In presenting the foregoing table and statements from girls, this commission does not take the position that the low wages of self-supporting girls is the sole contributing cause of their delinquency, realizing that there are thousands of girls who would endure the utmost hardships before yielding themselves to those who are ready to seduce them. The evidence as to the effect of wage conditions is taken from the girls themselves, who, perhaps lacking adequate moral training, have, in the extremities of their position, allowed themselves to be driven "the easiest way."[23]

In the vice investigation conducted by the Illinois State Senate, 50 girls in one day testified under oath, 45 of whom said that their downfall had been due to the lack of money. The foregoing evidence is the kind unfortunate girls would be likely to give. Nevertheless, making due allowances, this evidence tends to confirm reports of vice commissions whose purpose has been strictly scientific.

If a conservative estimate of the proportion of vice due to low wages of girls would be 10 to 15 per cent, it must not be concluded that this represents all of the baneful moral effect of poverty. Whatever the other non-economic causes of vice, they are aggravated where poverty exists. Not only is this so, but alleged other causes may be partly economic. Bad home conditions are due not only to the lack of moral discipline, but also to the lack of income. The average wage of the adult male wage-earner of that section of the United States lying east of the Rockies and north of Mason and Dixon's line is said to be about $600. Sometimes the wage is as low as $500, and in only a few instances as high as $750.[24] If wage-earning men attempt to support families on these incomes, it means that they are not able to provide adequately for their wives and children. If they do not attempt to do so, it means, taking men as they are, an increase in the army of men who support prostitution. Professor H.R. Seager has said that prostitution in aid of wages is the greatest disgrace of our civilization.[25] An accompanying disgrace lies in the fact that economic conditions and other factors prevent the average male wage-earner in so large a section of our country from fulfilling his desire for marriage and a home of the sort that makes for health and happiness.

Besides the low wages of women and men, other economic facts have their bearing upon sexual hygiene and morals. These facts may be grouped under the head of industrial stress and strain which is moral as well as physical. The underpaid factory or store girl is subject to constant fatigue. In the rush season in department stores, girls often depend upon opiates for dulling the nervous strain. No trade is free from its special physical strain. There are, moreover, many morally dangerous trades. Work as chambermaids in hotels is conspicuously perilous for girls. The Chicago Juvenile Protective Association says, "The majority of girls who work in hotels go wrong sooner or later." The modern department stores, which employ the majority of young working-girls, offer temptations. Mrs. Florence Kelley refers to work in these stores as "the most dangerous to morals and health, of all occupations into which children can go."[26] Of course, it may be said that a "good girl" will not go wrong. It may also be said that a good social order will not place even good girls daily under conditions that are liable to bring about a physical or moral breakdown. Closer analysis of human character reveals the fact that physical and moral health are more closely associated than we have hitherto believed them to be.

According to statistics about female offenders, domestic service is morally the most dangerous employment.[27] The reasons for this are two: the social ostracism and the loneliness, and the low grade of worker. Each of these causes augments the influence of the other. The application of industrial standards to this neglected form of work should lead to improvements.

For those dependent upon employment offices, the seeking of a job may involve moral danger. The practice of private employment bureaus in sending unsuspecting girls to immoral places under the pretext of finding legitimate employment is common. The director of the Municipal Employment Bureau in Portland says that, the managers of houses are sometimes so bold as to telephone to the bureau for girls, telling for what purpose the girls are wanted.[28] One of the private bureaus was detected several times cooperating in such practices. The menace of such places can scarcely be overestimated.

We may now conclude our review of the economic phases of social hygiene. Economic conditions to-day are under indictment as endangering the health and morals of working-girls and women. Moral delinquency may arise through temptations met and hardships endured at the place of work; through scanty wages, inadequate for daily necessities; through lack of sympathetic consideration on the part of employers; through the stupidity of the community in adhering to worn-out educational methods that do not train wage-earners for earning a livelihood; through lack of protective legislation in regard to hours and conditions of labor. As a matter of fact, each of these conditions has been found to be an accompaniment of vice; and taken all together they constitute an environment that makes clean living difficult. Against the dark background of modern industry should be portrayed the luxurious conditions that are apparently enjoyed by those who have taken "the easiest way." In ancient society the status of the prostitute was that of slave: to-day it is that of an industrial citizen.[29] If the program of social hygiene comprehended only talking about sex to working-girls--to laundry-girls, for example, who, after a day's work of ten hours at the machines, go at night to their boarding-houses where they wash dishes to eke out a living,--then this program would not be unlike the advice of a physician who tells a poor man with tuberculosis that he must go to the country for a year and live on cream and eggs.

Even in the case of wage-earning girls who adopt loose ways to satisfy extravagant desires, their tastes are established by women of the wealthy and middle classes. The leisure of these women is due to their wage-earning sisters, who in factories and mills make the cloth, prepare food-stuffs, and do all sorts of tasks that formerly kept women of the upper classes at home. Through the instinct of imitation, combined with the American feeling of democracy, the habits of the well-to-do determine the ambition of many a working-girl.

Other factors are industrial arrangements which segregate men in construction and lumber camps for a part of the year, and then, without providing for their further employment, turn them loose into cities where only saloons welcome them and cash their checks, and where disease-infected lodging-houses are their only places of abode. Furthermore, standing armies take thousands of able-bodied men out of normal industrial relationships, and keep them in camps that become the congregating places of prostitutes.

The most hopeful phase of the whole problem that it lies within the power of the State to transform the industrial environment through progressive legislation. The law cannot form character, but it can protect that which has been developed through voluntary effort. Vice is partly a by-product of industrial chaos which can be eradicated by industrial organization. When working-people can establish themselves more generally in homes of their own,--"every man under his vine, and under his fig tree," as it were,--then they will be able to give more time to their children, and will perhaps cooperate better in the program for sex instruction.

Economic improvements should include a minimum wage for women, and one for
men based upon the needs of a family; the eight-hour day; insurance
against sickness, old age, and accidents; relief of unemployment; one
day's rest in seven for all continuous industries; industrial education
compulsory for all children; abolition of child labor; and amelioration of
conditions under which women work.

When wage standards are raised, there arises the problem concerning those
who cannot earn a living wage. "Who will pay poor, ignorant Mary Konovsky
more than $6.90 a week?" is a question asked by a manufacturer during a
minimum-wage discussion in New York State. The reply is, If Mary is really
not worth more, she must be sent by the State to an industrial school
until she can earn her living; and if she should be proved to be mentally
deficient (as about 50 per cent of prostitutes are said to be), then she
must be placed in an institution where she can be humanely and permanently
cared for. The impossible alternatives are that she should be denied a
living wage when she can earn it, or that she should be allowed to drift,
in danger of becoming the prey of vicious men.

Meanwhile, before the machinery of a full legislative program can be set
to work, the field is open for voluntary philanthropic endeavor. Welfare
work in stores and factories that is done by some one who acts, not as a
detective with condescending side interests in welfare, but
whole-heartedly and sympathetically can avail much. Real social work in
business establishments should be profitable to employers as well as to
employees. The aim of all public and private effort should be to make
industry not the occasion of stumbling, but what it should be, the
universal means of progress.

NOTES:

[2] ***Statistical Abstract of U.S.***, p. 163. (1911.)

[3] ***Woman and Child Wage-Earners in U.S.***, vol. IX, p. 20; "History of Women in Industry."

[4] ***A New Conscience and an Ancient Evil***, chap. I.

[5] ***A Trade School for Girls***, U.S. Bureau of Education, Bulletin no. 17, pp. 52 ***ff.*** (1913.)

[6] Portland, Oregon, Vice Commission, ***Report***, p. 188. (1913.)

[7] ***Social Basis of Religion.***

[8] Social Survey Committee of Consumers' League of Oregon, ***Report***, pp. 21, 22.

[9] ***Ibid.***, p. 24.

[10] Massachusetts Commission on Minimum Wage Boards, ***Report***, pp. 51, 114, 157.

[11] *Ibid.*, p. 191.

[12] *Report* of Massachusetts Commission, as above cited, p. 188.

[13] *Ibid.*, p. 114.

[14] *Woman and Child Wage-Earners*, vol. V. The cities included were Boston, New York, Philadelphia, Chicago, St. Paul, Minneapolis, and St. Louis.

[15] By "adrift" is meant the condition of a self-supporting woman who is alone or of a widow with children to support.

[16] *Report* of Massachusetts Commission, p. 213.

[17] *Ibid.*, p. 222.

[18] *Report* of Portland Vice Commission, p. 165.

[19] *Morning Oregonian*, July 24, 1913.

[20] Referred to on p. 211 of the *Report* of the Massachusetts Commission

on Minimum Wage Boards.

[21] **Woman and Child Wage-Earners**, vol. XV, pp. 81, **ff.**; "Relation of Occupation and Criminality of Women."

[22] **Report** of Portland Vice Commission, p. 176.

[23] **Report** of Portland Vice Commission, p. 176.

[24] Scott Nearing, **Wages in the United States**, pp. 208, **ff.**

[25] **American Labor Legislation Review**, vol. III, no. 1, p. 88.

[26] **Social Diseases**, vol. III, no. 3, p. 9.

[27] See Portland Vice Commission **Report**, p. 193; also **Woman and Child Wage-Earners**, vol. XV.

[28] Portland Vice Commission **Report**, p. 192.

[29] E.R. Seligman, **The Social Evil**, Introduction.

CHAPTER VI

RECREATIONAL PHASES

By Lebert Howard Weir

This chapter is in no sense an attempt to discuss pathologic sex problems, but rather to show the necessity of providing facilities for normal, wholesome living for all the people during their leisure time. This will solve many of the vexing sex problems.

At the outset, it is important to contrast the 27,000,000 hours a year, during which the school has charge of all the children, with the 135,000,000 hours at the children's free disposal. Yet we are inclined to charge the schools with the responsibilities of many failures in the physical and moral make-up of growing boys and girls. The greater part of the education of the boys and girls is received outside of school through the various activities which fill up these 135,000,000 hours a year. Society has, therefore, a great responsibility in directing the activities of the free time of young people.

People employed in the home, store, factory, shop, or office, in a year of 365 days spend about 2880 hours of this time in sleep. Taking the average working-day as nine hours and the number of working-days in the year as 300, excluding Sundays and holidays, each person is employed in needful occupations 2700 hours during the year. Out of the working-days, a total of 2100 hours are at each person's disposal to use as he sees fit. Of the remaining 60 days, 15 hours of each day are for free use,--or a total of nearly 35 per cent of the entire year. What are the children, young people, and adults doing with this time?

One answer is found in the records of the juvenile court, in rescue homes, in reformatories, in the police and criminal courts, in jails and penitentiaries, in hospitals for the treatment of venereal diseases, the insane and feeble-minded; another in the fallen women (and men, too), of whom so much has been said of late; another in the crowded saloons and busy restaurants in the heart of the city, with their music, bright lights, food, liquor, and overdressed, painted women with their consorts; still another in the billiard-rooms and the moving-picture theaters.

The extent to which people of all ages and races resort to the moving-picture show is known by few people. In Portland, Oregon, a weekly attendance of 5000 is reported for a house with a seating capacity of 175; a weekly attendance of 3500 for a house seating 75; a weekly attendance of 25,000 for a house seating 500. Another with a seating capacity of 567 reports a weekly attendance of 22,000. The attendance of all the moving-picture houses in any city is a startling revelation of the use of the time of the people.

All forms of leisure-time consumption are offshoots of the one great common meeting-place of all the people, the street. The street is more than an avenue for traffic. It is the social meeting-place of many of the inhabitants. It is the playground of nearly all the children. Its glitter and glare, its lights and shadows and care-free spirit, attract boys and girls. They come as moths flutter about the candle flame and often with equally disastrous results. The call of the street is irresistible. It is the simplest, most convenient avenue for the satisfaction of that hunger for pleasure, excitement, amusement, and recreation, common to all ages, all races, and both sexes. It is the avenue for the spontaneous outpouring of the spirit of democracy. No matter how thickly the city may scatter its playgrounds, its athletic fields, boating and swimming centers and recreation buildings, the street will always have to be reckoned with as the one great all-engulfing factor in the use of the leisure time of the people.

Surely the possibilities for good or evil are infinite when the spirit of youth and age play free, willingly receiving impressions on every hand. Unfortunately, in the majority of cases the ministry in this field of infinite character-building possibilities has fallen into the hands of men who for the most part reckon its possibilities only in terms of the nickels, dimes, and dollars that pass over the bar or counter or through the box office. Many of them conceive low opinions of the recreation desires of the people, furnishing the lurid, the *risque*, the bold, the daring forms of entertainment, or coupling it with other lines of business, as in the case of the saloon, with unfortunate social results.

Can the city afford the commercial exploitations of so much of this valuable time? The answer must be that it can afford it only when the ideals of the men conducting these various forms of amusement are as high as the best that the community would demand if managing similar institutions. The saloon proprietor is not interested primarily in the physical and moral welfare of his patrons or in the general social welfare of the city. He provides various forms of recreation to increase the patronage of the bar; it is an unwritten law that those who avail themselves of the card-tables, of the pool- and billiard-tables, the moving-picture shows in the saloons, and who hear the music, must patronize the bar. Thirty-six per cent of the pool and billiard licenses are held by men holding saloon licenses, and in all the large pool- and billiard-halls, especially in the center of the city, not connected directly with saloons, liquor is served upon the demand of the patrons. The evil of the situation is significant when it is remembered that the larger percentage of the patrons of those places are men under twenty-five years of age. Profanity is common, and usually gambling is permitted. Often these pool- and billiard-parlors are the "hang-outs" of vicious, depraved young men who live upon the earnings of unfortunate women. This use of the leisure time of men is physically, morally, and socially dangerous and should not be permitted.

The public skating-rink is fairly free from objectionable features, but boys and girls attending without proper chaperons often form undesirable acquaintances. Women of the street and their male companions often attend. Juvenile court officials are aware of the immoralities springing from this source.

The amusement parks present almost unlimited possibilities for the formation of undesirable acquaintances. The fact that they are open in the evening, and not lighted in all parts, the presence of cafes where liquors can be had, inadequate police protection, the secrecy possible through the presence of large crowds, the size of the parks, the distance from the homes in the city, and the unchaperoned attendance of large crowds of young people, all make amusement parks dangerous without closer supervision by public authorities.

In former days the road-house ministered to the legitimate needs of wayfaring travelers. To-day the name "road-house" is synonymous with the "bawdy-house" of the city. Located just beyond the borders of towns and cities, beyond police supervision, catering to men and women who desire secrecy for their revels and orgies, the road-house is one of the worst possible institutions now ministering to the leisure time of the people.

In some sections of this country, the public excursion, both by land and water, is as bad as the road-house. Instead of being a time of relaxation and recreation, a time of freedom from cares of the workaday life and enjoyment of pure air, sunshine, and beauties of nature, and of fine social relationships of people, the excursions have become dissipations of physical and moral energy. With proper supervision and with proper standards on the part of promoters of transportation companies, the public excursion can be a fine constructive factor in the use of the leisure time of the people.

Festivals and carnivals conducted by the people of a community, commemorative of national holidays or of historical events or of religious life, are often admirable. But whenever the festival or carnival becomes a commercial enterprise for the purpose of attracting crowds to the city, for advertisement and for gain by merchants and hotel proprietors, young people are in danger. The city becomes the mecca for undesirable men and women who prey upon the susceptibilities of the people, animated by the festival spirit. The hotels are the temporary homes of women of the street. Every large festival of this kind has been followed by social evils of the most virulent type. Many a girl and many a boy, yielding to the influences of the abandonment of the crowd, take the first step in sexual vice. This type of festival is not socially profitable to a community, where the commercial aim and purpose predominates. The commercial exploitation of the recreation and social needs of the people is usually productive of sexual immorality.

A characteristic feature of American life is the club, union, society, or order spontaneously formed by the people. No matter what the fundamental purposes of these groups may be, whether for protection against sickness, accident, and industrial evils, whether for the study of art, music, and literature, or for the promotion of physical activities, the primary bond that brings the group together and holds it together is the social instinct of mankind.

Those which administer to the play and recreation life of their members most efficiently are strongest. The dances, card parties, lectures, entertainments, and other social activities conducted by such groups are usually under the best kind of social control, far better than any type of commercial amusement and perhaps better than most public-supervised amusements. The strength is in the comparative smallness of the group, the personal acquaintance of the members, the presence of older people with the young, and the existence of individual and group responsibility and ideals. Far better social control would result if all public dances and public skating-rinks and excursions were conducted on this group or society basis.

One field of neglected social activity is the home as a recreation and social center. The day of the "party" seems to be past. Parents have thus lost one strong hold on the character development of their children. Thousands of parents in the modern city have lost the social spirit of the home because of crowded living conditions, but there are also thousands, especially in the Western cities, who still have individual homes; every such home should be the primary social and recreation center for adolescent boys and girls. The revival of the small group social in the home for the young people would be a constructive contribution to some of the moral problems of the young.

In the leisure-time activities of children, the Sunday supplement or "funny sheet" of the newspaper is of importance. The funny sheet appeals not so much through humor as through glaring color and grotesque pictures which violate every canon of color combination and of art. Exaggerated types of mischievous children and freakish adults, and equally freakish and unthinkable mechanical devices, are favorite subjects. Disobedience of children, premature and unnatural childish love-affairs, domestic infelicity, the privileges and advantages of bachelorhood are paraded Sunday after Sunday before the susceptible minds of millions of children.

*   *   *   *   *

Multitudinous as are the private agencies administering to the leisure-time activities of all the people, neither the commercial amusements nor the numerous spontaneous private organizations answer all the requirements of social and recreative needs of the people. On the one hand, commercial amusements, while used and enjoyed by masses of the people, have been objects of danger and distrust because of their anti-social effects. On the other hand, the private society, club, order, and organization are essentially narrow, and formed with other purposes and ideals in view than ministering to the social and recreative needs and desires of the people. The providing of ample facilities for the fullest and most wholesome use of the leisure time of the people is a community responsibility, just as important to the public welfare as a system of public education.

This community sense of responsibility did not in the beginning have the wide constructive vision which characterizes it to-day. It was designed first as a corrective of pathological social ills, especially relative to childhood and youth. Congestion in the modern city, an incident and a result of specialization and expansion of American industrial and commercial life, caused living conditions inimical to the health and morals of all the people. As usual the children suffered most. Deprived of light, air, wholesome living quarters, play space, and the advantages of a real home, they fell easy victims to disease, sickness, death, and, what is worse, to the disease and death of ideals and morals. Juvenile faults and crimes increased at an alarming rate. The therapy of play was applied. It was soon found, however, that the great mission of playgrounds was not as a therapeutic agent, but as a preventive and constructive force. The movement took on large, positive, constructive aims, purposes, and ideals. It expanded into the playground and recreation movement, with emphasis upon the latter, aiming to provide for and direct the leisure-time activities of all the people. Play was restored as the right of every child, without which no wholesome physical, mental, and moral growth is possible.

As constructively related to other great social problems, the playground and recreation movement was found almost universally applicable. Sexual immorality and the white-slave traffic are combated by recreation centers where young women obtain under normal conditions the highest ideals and satisfy the spirit of youth, which is the sign of life itself.

The scope of this larger movement is as follows: It promotes the establishment of playgrounds within walking distance of every child; athletic and sport fields for older boys and girls and for men and women; boating and swimming centers and parks for the use of all; recreation and social centers in municipal recreation buildings and in school buildings, where all the people of a community, irrespective of race or creed, may find opportunity for the fullest possible recreation and social life; it promotes school and municipal camps, tramping-clubs, and other activities that cultivate the habit of outdoor life; physical education and athletics in the schools that reach every child, instead of a few as now; it stands for school playgrounds, in connection with every school; it seeks to provide facilities through which musical, literary, dramatic, and artistic talents of the people may find encouragement and expression, and for a constructive social supervision of all commercial amusements.

Yet playgrounds and recreation centers are not free from social dangers. Many of the moral dangers of commercial amusements may arise in municipally owned and managed systems of recreation. In fact public playgrounds have become such moral menaces as to warrant their closure in the interests of public welfare. Some of the worst cases of sexual immorality coming to the juvenile courts arise in public playgrounds. This is the result of bringing large numbers of young people into a common play place without the most careful supervision, guidance, and direction. The physical growth and health, the morals, the happiness, and the ideals of citizenship of great masses of the people are so deeply involved in the right use of the leisure time of the people that to conduct their activities in any way but according to the highest standards is a civic crime.

CHAPTER VII

EDUCATIONAL PHASES

By Edward Octavius Sisson

The education of youth as it exists has a great gap wherever the subjects of reproduction and sex are concerned. Children are taught at home many things about every other part of their lives, but usually nothing about this; at school they learn the anatomy and physiology of bones and muscles, of sense-organs, and nervous system, of glands and alimentary canal, of respiration and circulation; but a sudden silence falls just before sex is reached. We study everything about life except its origin, and in ignoring that we lose a most fascinating and beautiful field of inquiry, an essential part of knowledge, and a vital element in moral intelligence.[30]

The aims of sex education may be stated in the main as follows:--

(1) The first aim is individual prudence. Every normal human being must undergo crucial tests and solve vital problems in his own sex life. The most beautiful successes of life and its most conspicuous failures are both exceedingly frequent in the realm of sex. The conditions of the sexual life are sufficiently alike in all normal cases so that the experience of the race is valuable to the individual in meeting his own problems. Each child as he passes onward through youth to maturity is treading a road new to him, not lacking in danger and pitfalls, nor without opportunities for great reward. Education must give him all the available advance information concerning the road he is to travel.

(2) The second aim is general intelligence. Sex is a universal element in all living beings, with the exception of the very lowest; it pervades the life of the spirit as well as the life of the body. No man, therefore, can be intelligent concerning things in general without a clear, definite and accurate knowledge of the fundamental facts of sex. One of the strongest new visions concerning sex is the marvelous way in it ramifies into all fields of thought and action. Not a few of the most eminent workers in modern science incline to consider all aspects of human life, including even religion itself, as emanations or processes from the sex basis. Such in particular are G. Stanley Hall in America and Freud in Germany. Without going to such extremes we may still recognize the fact that in all sorts of physical and psychic problems in morals, religion, and sociology, sex plays an important part and must be understood if we are to grasp the situation and its meaning.[31]

(3) The third aim is social enlightenment. The human spirit in our own day is manifestly addressing itself to the solution of the special social problems which involve the sexual life of men. Three of these problems may be specified: (a) The so-called "social evil," including not merely prostitution, but also all other forms of waste and injury through sexual errors; (b) the problem of family life, including marriage and the rearing of children, as well as pathological aspects such as desertion and divorce; (c) the vast problem of eugenics or race culture.

In all these fields the problems of sex are involved. Men and women who desire to bear their whole burden as members of a progressive society must contribute to the solution of these great social problems, and to do this wisely must know something about the basic facts of sex life.[32]

The first and basic part of sex education is bodily regimen: children and youth must live an abundant, vigorous, wholesome physical life.[33] Cities have threatened to be the "graves of the human species" in this respect.

Sedentary life chokes and misdirects the currents of nervous energy and the very circulation of the blood. The lad who plays vigorously, even violently; who can "get his second wind," turn a handspring, do a good cross-country run, swim the river, possesses a great bulwark of defense against sexual vice, especially in its secret forms.

The revival of play, of play for all, boys and girls, weak as well as strong, is one of the most hopeful movements on foot to-day. Let us base our promotions from grade to grade, and especially for "graduation" from school, partly upon physical tests, requiring each student to make of himself physically, not a record-breaking athlete, but the best that can be made out of the stuff in him.

Food, sleep, clothing, bathing, fresh air,--all these are vital also; whatever turns the flow and thrill of life into wholesome channels, abolishes indolence, stagnation, morbidity, and fosters abundance of bodily life,--such is the regimen of sex health.

No bodily regimen can be effective without mental control. Nowhere does mind affect body more immediately and powerfully than in the realm of sex. The educator has two great tasks in this respect: first to improve the general environment in which the young must live and develop. As things are, our streets, store-windows, books and magazines, and especially public amusements, such as theaters and dance halls, abound in sexual suggestion and stimulation.[34] These agencies stimulate an excessive stream of sexual desire, with all its physical accompaniments, in boys and men: the natural and inevitable result is an overwhelming impulse toward illicit satisfaction in self-abuse or sexual immorality. Society in self-defense and the interest of its youth must wage war upon this mercenary exploiting of the sex impulse. Licentious thinking is the great foe of continence; the saying of Jesus may be paraphrased thus with physiological correctness: "He that looketh upon a woman to lust after her hath already committed the sexual act in his *nervous system*."

Hence, the second task in this connection is to arouse and arm the youth against the lusts of the mind, and lead him in a resolute fight for mastery over his own thoughts. "Do not harbor in your mind anything you would fear to have your enemies know, or blush to have your friends know," is a good motto for boys and youth.

When we come to instruction in matters of reproduction and sex, the first principle is that it should be given in organic relation with the rest of life and thought. It arises naturally in two main connections: in response to the child's own questions and problems; and as part and parcel of biological science. The common questions of the little child, "Where does the baby come from?" or perhaps even earlier, "How does the hen make the eggs?"--an actual question of a four-year-old--are the signal and the open door for easy and natural enlightenment. Seize the opportunity: tell the truth, as simply and briefly as possible, and the beginning is made; watch for and utilize all such opportunities, as they come, and the main road of the task is marked out; shock is minimized, if not eliminated, mutual confidence is engendered, and a priceless reward may be won. But if at that first question we falter, quibble, blush, lie, jest, or repel, we have entered the wrong road which leads eternally astray. Let no question ever be either ignored or neglected, least of all repelled. It is the golden opportunity for parent, teacher, or friend. To guarantee against the child seeking promiscuous and irresponsible sources of information, let his questions ever find the warmest welcome and kindest response at the parent's knee.[35]

Now the movements of the child's own mind in matters of sex and reproduction may either be actual questions more or less explicit, or they may be subtler seekings for light,--hints, vague inquiries, gropings after what he cannot phrase or hesitates to utter; these inward stirrings are vital, and the alert and sympathetic and patient parent can in the main perceive them and bring them to light. But success need not be hoped for in this respect unless first the beginnings are attended to; uncounted parents can testify to the infinite difficulty of breaking to the boy or girl the silence long practiced with the child. Nor will occasional or spasmodic fits of interest and action by the parent achieve much; Emerson's proverb holds inflexibly here; "What wilt thou have?" quoth God; "pay for it and take it." Pay we must in time, in thought, in perseverance and patience, in study of the problems and self-preparation for the task. Happily the progress of sex hygiene among adults is yearly increasing the number of fathers and mothers who are awake and active.

We have spoken of meeting the motions of the child, as though the educator might never need to take the initiative; in all probability that might be true in an ideal state. As things are it would be unsafe to rely absolutely upon questions; the parent and on occasion other educators must take the initiative in some cases. In doing so, however, the most scrupulous care should be taken to be sure that the mind of the learner is ready for the particular instruction.

*   *   *   *   *

In biological instruction what is needed is not an artificial appendix or addendum, but simply that we should cease to mutilate science by omitting its most fruitful and essential elements. Nature study for little children is the first available field; it should begin even before the kindergarten age, with the simplest and easiest observations, and proceed by gentle gradations of progress; it finds abundant and fascinating material in growing plants, eggs, brooding chickens, kittens, puppies, and, best of all, the new baby, where the home questions and the nature study meet in a profound emotional and intellectual experience.[36]

The botany, zooelogy, physiology, and hygiene the upper grades and the high school the natural mediums for further scientific treatment.[37] It will probably be found advisable to separate the sexes for this part of the work, and have boys taught by men and girls by women. Not a few high schools and colleges are already carrying on such instruction with entire success.

It seems quite clear that the school must set itself, wisely, indeed, but also resolutely and effectively, to provide clear, true, scientific knowledge of the origin of life and the laws of sex. The educator can, must, and will answer truly and purely, all questions in these matters on which the child and youth are now left to random, miscellaneous, clandestine sources, and get vile, false, and pernicious answers.

*   *   *   *   *

As childhood passes into youth and the pubertal changes begin, the objective curiosity of the earliest years passes gradually into the intense concern of personal problems. The general principle is the same: do not drag in the subject of sex and reproduction, but do not evade or ignore it when it appears; deal with it truly, purely, honestly, fearlessly, as an essential and organic part of truth and life.

The safe and happy outcome in these personal problems can be guaranteed in only one way--that the young person should be able to turn with complete confidence and little embarrassment to some trusted and intimate counselor, preferably the parent, but otherwise physician, pastor, older friend, with whom he has already discussed sexual questions, and who he knows will receive his advances with sympathy, answer his questions with frankness and intelligence, and hold his confidence sacred. Happy the youth or maiden who has such a guide in the crises of unfolding powers and perils.

The chief problem of this part of the education is the accurate and timely adaptation of what is taught to the needs of the successive periods of development. Hence chronological or "calendar" age and school grade are both unreliable guides to the educator: a group of fifteen-year-old boys, or of eighth grade boys, includes some who are children not yet entered upon pubescence, others who are mature,--that is, have attained the power of reproduction,--and still others who are in process of change. These three groups cannot be treated identically; each period has its own peculiar needs. The problem of sorting out the individuals and meeting the needs of each group is difficult because of our traditional neglect of the whole task. But of any particular lesson we may agree with him who says, "Better a year too early than an hour too late."

The earliest safeguard, rather regimen than instruction, is the inculcation of the idea and habit of "Hands off" the sex organs. The little child is taught this by his mother, and it becomes second nature. The pre-pubescent boy and girl may receive some slight but impressive additional perception as to the danger of meddling in any way. They should also be warned strictly against any other person who offers to tamper with their sex organs or adjacent parts of the body. Let them understand that they are justified in any means of defense, the fist, a club, or a stone; and that the offender is forever damned by his act and must never again be trusted; and, of course, that they should at once lay the whole case before their parents or other persons in authority.

The special instruction of the pre-pubescent and pubescent periods is as yet by no means fully agreed upon among experts. We can give here only a few points that seem fairly clear.

(1) Girls should know in advance enough of the general facts of menstruation so that the onset of the period may not cause, as it now does in thousands of cases, shock and sometimes dangerous errors of conduct. They should also know that the sexual nature of men is active and aggressive instead of passive and defensive as in the woman; and that hence the woman must in general take the leading part in the control of the sexual relation, or, at least, of those preliminary intimacies that

tend to culminate in sexual union. If it be contended that this is a delicate and difficult idea to convey, liable to be exaggerated and to produce false attitudes, the answer is that if difficulty is to deter us we may as well stop the whole task of sex education before we begin; and moreover that the disasters now resulting from ignorance are ten times worse than any probable results of instruction.

This sexual difference means not only that the girl must be intolerant of improper advances, but also that for her own sake and that of her sister women she must beware of conduct, attitudes, or forms of dress that tend unduly to excite the sexual impulses in boys and men.

In view of the enormous morbidity and mortality inflicted upon innocent women and their children by sexual disease, the girl should learn the main facts concerning the nature, effects, and incidence of gonorrhea and syphilis. Health certificates of prospective bridegrooms will probably be more easily enforced if such intelligence becomes general. The time for such instruction is difficult to state, and would vary with the social environment; probably late adolescence would be early enough in most cases; earlier information is indispensable for girls who by reason of their economic or social status are peculiarly exposed to sexual temptation and danger.

Training for motherhood, a great gap in our educational system, is a closely related theme, of incomparable importance, but beyond the scope of this work.

(2) Boys should learn early the rewards of continence: that the conservation of the sexual secretions is the indispensable condition of manly growth in stature, muscular powers, voice, heart, and brain. They should learn the possibility and healthiness of continence--always understanding that mental continence is the prerequisite of physical continence.

They should know in good time that nocturnal emissions are quite normal, when not too frequent, and indicate not lost manhood or the danger of it, but merely the fact that the sexual glands are now for the first time all developed and active. This is one of the simplest and most commonplace facts in the whole range of sex knowledge, yet, through ignorance of it, unknown multitudes of boys have suffered anxiety sometimes amounting to terror, have become moody and dejected, lost interest in work and studies; and finally thousands of them, ashamed to ask counsel or enlightenment from any decent source, have had recourse to the venereal quack, who so artfully spreads his snares for them in daily paper and widely circulated pamphlet. Once the victim is in his hands there is almost no limit to the evil that may result.[38] High-school principals tell of watching the faces of their boys during a lecture on sex hygiene and noting the visible signs of relief and new hope when the lecturer explained the true nature and meaning of emissions.

So far as the so-called "sexual necessity" is concerned, let boys understand that it is unknown among animals; that its completest embodiment is found in degenerates and imbeciles; and that athletes, thinkers, priests, scholars, warriors, the finest men of every type, hold their passions strictly subject to their wills. Let them know that the world is well supplied with wretches whom this very "sexual necessity" has robbed of their precious virile powers, but that the cases of impotence through chastity are certainly unproved and probably non-existent except in the imagination of people who want to believe in them. And finally that numberless fathers of big healthy families were as chaste as the wives who bore their children.

Boys should learn that the man who insists on premarital sexual necessity has two roads open to him--one that of the libertine and seducer, the most contemptible of creatures; the other that of the whore-follower, whom nature perpetually menaces with vile and pestilential plagues, making him a misery to himself and menace to all clean persons who associate with him, especially his future wife and unborn children.

This involves, at least for the present state of society, some information regarding the two chief venereal diseases: that all prostitutes, professional or otherwise, are sooner or later infected, and that no reglementation can give security. They should know something of the horrors of syphilis, its loathsomeness, its extraordinary power to penetrate to the physiological Holy of Holies, poison the germ cells, and damn in advance the unborn children of its victim. They must know the fatal treachery of gonorrhea: how it lurks unsuspected in the victim who supposes himself cured, and strikes, like a bolt out of clear sky, blinding newborn infants, and robbing innocent wives of motherhood, health, or life itself.

To object to this instruction because it is gruesome, or because it may seem like intimidation, is sentimentalism: in this matter, as elsewhere in the realm of knowledge, the truth should scare no one who does not need to be scared. It is better to be safe than sorry; and it is better to be scared than syphilitic. "I dare do all that may become a man," says Macbeth; "who dares do more is none"; let a man dare if he will with his own body, aye, his own soul; he is but a coward who does not shrink from buying voluptuous moments with the hazard of wife and child. Hydrophobia is far less perilous than venereal disease, and if one hundredth as many were attacked by it the world would be placarded with scarlet danger signs; the man who decried the precautions as intimidation would be shut up in a home for imbeciles. If this is intimidation, let us have more of it.

Above all, boys should learn the beauty and glory of the true relation of the sexes; the bond of love and unity between man and woman truly married--in soul as well as body. As he cherishes and vindicates the honor of his father and mother and sisters, so should he be taught to use his intelligence and heart to hold sacred in youth the powers and functions that will enable him to become in turn husband and father, to give a clean soul and body in marriage to a pure woman, and to pass on the germ of life to the children of his body. A few lessons on heredity will show him that he is but the steward of an inheritance that has come down from a thousand ancestors and may well be perpetuated through generations to come. Prudence is good; but no narrow selfish motive will meet the need. The lad who is "good" merely for the sake of his own skin is usually a poor creature; the finest lad--who might perhaps hazard his own individual fate--will refuse to gamble with the souls and bodies of those others who shall be his own flesh and blood. No virtue is safe that is not enthusiastic: and only altruism is truly enthusiastic.

The boy and girl, now young man and young woman, must both learn that prostitution is a social sin:[39] the "scarlet woman" has been truly called the eternal priestess bearing the sins of humanity. This is a vast theme; we have got beyond the realm of mere sex education;--but truth is one, and life is one, and neither logic nor humanity will consent to our stopping short of the whole truth. Social intelligence--the illumination of man's life with man--the scientific and spiritual comprehension of the apostolic dictum, "We are all members one of another"--and "if one member suffer, all members suffer with it"--these are the great arrears of education. But there never was a time when the spirit of man moved so rapidly forward as here and now, and the movement for sex education is but one striking phase of the great advance.

NOTES:

[30] An examination of tables of contents and indexes of standard school texts in nature study and biology will reveal the almost universal absence of all ideas relating to sex and reproduction. There are two or three recent exceptions.

[31] G. Stanley Hall, *Educational Problems*, vol. I, pp. 388-97, Thomson and Geddes, *Problems of Sex*, pp. 5-17.

[32] Thomson and Geddes, *op. cit.*, pp. 46-52; Saleeby, *Parenthood and Race Culture*; Morrow, *Social Diseases and Marriage; Hall, Educational Problems*, vol. I, pp. 424-43.

[33] Fisher, *National Vitality*; Hall, *Youth*, chaps. II, V, VI, XII.

[34] "What makes a Magazine?" *Twentieth Century Magazine*, September, 1912, pp. 11-20; *The Exploitation of Pleasure.* Russell Sage Foundation.

[35] See Mrs. Woodallen Chapman, *The Moral Problem of the Children*, esp. pp. 61-93. Also the chapter in this book on the education of children.

[36] An epoch-marking book in this field is Miss Torelle's *Plant and Animal Children and How They Grow.* (Heath.) See also pamphlet, *The Origin of Life*, by R.E. Blount. (Scott, Foresman & Co.)

[37] "The Teaching of Sex in Schools and Colleges," *Social Diseases*, October, 1911. Addresses by G. Stanley Hall, Maurice A. Bigelow, Josiah

Strong, Charles W. Eliot, and Mary Putnam Blount, *Sexual Reproduction in Animals: the Purpose and Methods of teaching it.* Proceedings N.E.A.,

1912, pp. 1324-27.

[38] Hall, G.S., *Adolescence*, vol. I, pp. 459-62.

[39] Jane Addams, *A New Conscience and an Ancient Evil.*

CHAPTER VIII

TEACHING PHASES: FOR CHILDREN

By William Greenleaf Eliot, Jr.

My children when they were little were fascinated with a book which their mother used to read to them, called *Mother Nature and Her Helpers.* Each chapter or lesson was made up of interesting information and ideas suggested by the pictures. At the head of the first chapter was a picture of a mother sitting by a cradle with every surrounding and circumstance of humble, happy home life. Succeeding chapters were upon the cradle and the home of plants and animals. Ovaries of plants and nests of birds and squirrels were all set forth in terms of the child's experience of home life, home-building, home-protecting, and feeding the baby. Doubtless the design of the author was to lead the child to an understanding and appreciation of its own home life and love by showing it home life in its origins and elements. But an equally important implication lay in the fact that the child was brought into its intimacy with plant and animal life along the angle of its own human experience and of its own home ideals. After such an introduction to the homes of plants and animals, whenever it should seem best to apprise the child of the details of plant and animal reproduction, the additional facts would instantly find their places in close relation to facts already familiar and already related to his highest childish affections and ideals.

For the basis of sexual instruction for a child should be the difference, not the similarity between man and animals. If the basis is made the similarity between man and animals, the child, as time goes on and as its own sexual life increasingly awakens, may tend to imitate animals, may attempt to justify the natural and unrestrained promiscuousness of its own instincts, may justify unrestrained sexual life in the name of nature as against the alleged artificialities of civilization. The basis must be human, not animal; moral, not biological.

Biology goes far to explain humanity, but the interpretation is found in the spiritual affections, experiences, and implications of family life. The family life of animals is constituted of animal instinct freely followed. The family life of man would be ruined by the free following of animal instinct. There is a distinct danger in all so-called sex instruction of children which makes plant and animal life the norm.

The definite and clean instruction of children in the physical facts of reproduction may rightly and wisely begin with the simple facts, anatomical and functional, of plants and animals; but it is important that a true philosophy lie back of this instruction. Man is not only a higher order of mammalia; he is a worshiper of God and capable of practicing his presence. And from this base our instruction to children, drawn from the anatomical and functional life of plants and animals, must always subserve the moral, the spiritual superiority of man and the human family.

The little child will understand and even idealize plant and animal life if he learns of plant and animal life first in human terms. His moral development is menaced if this process is reversed so that a counter-tendency is set up,--a tendency to interpret the human functions in animal terms. It is better for the child to humanize animal relationships than to animalize human relationships,--and this can be achieved only through a constant observance of the human basis in the sexual as indeed in all phases of a child's education. The little book which I mentioned at the beginning does just this,--it introduces the child to the home life of animals, it interprets animal life in ideal terms. It lays a basis for relating later information of sex functions to the home life of plants and animals. At the proper time in a child's development, he is prepared to place a true and intelligent value upon the differences between the home life of animals and the home life of human beings, and to justify intelligently and with full consent of mind and sanction of conscience the differences of sexual practice as between plants and animals on the one hand and human beings on the other. He is prepared to see that it is enough for the sex life of plants and animals that it be physically and biologically normal. It is not enough for the true and ideal family life of man that the sex relation should be biologically normal. It must be morally normal--normal, that is, to the highest human interests.

The more concrete and detailed problems of method would not be serious if every child's mind were a blank or even if its instincts were analogous to normal animals. But neither is the case, and the problem of method and means of instruction is therefore amazingly complicated. If the sex life of a child were analogous to that of normal animals, it would not awaken at all until puberty. And if the child's mind were a blank on sex matters, it need only be kept from the invasion of wrong ideas from outside. But the sex life of a child begins long before puberty,--both physically and mentally. In the child, the physical signs are more or less detached from the mental signs,--at this or that phase of a child's life, the one or the other may have precedence; but the two are subtly interrelated, and tend to contribute to each other. In the human being a sex life that is normal, both biologically and morally, is an achievement; not a thing which would take care of itself if the child were left alone and merely kept ignorant of the abnormal. The human child is born abnormal,--that is to say, with latent possibilities of sexual abnormality, physical and mental,--and this by virtue of the mere fact that he is not only with animals a creature of instinct, but with humanity a being with ideas.

This statement is doubtless oftener true of the sex life of boy children than of girl children; but it is a fact and a very important fact, and it lies at the bottom of the problem when we come to consider the details of instructional method. If it were not for these facts, it would make no difference who imparted sex information to the child, so the facts were accurately told; and it would make no difference what facts were given, or at what age the child received them, if no lies were conveyed. But because the child's physical and mental sex life awakens early, and because every child has latent tendencies to abnormality and latent responsiveness to the abnormal, it is of critical importance that we decide who shall teach the individual child, when the child shall be informed, and what the child shall be told. It is of critical importance because, if the instruction comes wrongly, we may, even with good intentions, contribute to the very abnormality that we wish to forefend or overcome. With some children we could perhaps safely take chances so far as the self-awakening sex life is concerned if we did not know that it is impossible, without more harm than good to keep the child from such perfectly normal relations with other children as almost certainly will expose it to disastrous misinformation a suggestion.

Whatever ought to be said of the importance of the home tradition and ideals and the general physical and moral regimen of the child (and these are of supreme importance), the facts of the last two paragraphs lay the ground for this general statement: that in the case of a child whose moral and sexual environment has been bad and perverting, proper sex instruction cannot make matters worse, whereas in the best families much harm may arise from the lack of such instruction.

If any information is imparted to the child at all, the first instruction should properly come from one or other of the child's parents. It is sometimes the case that opportunity for the first information is presented when the child asks questions. And the supposed question of the child is, "Where did the baby come from?" Our course would be much smoother if every child asked its mother or father this question, or if every child began with this particular question, or if every child asked any question at all. Sometimes the child asks the nurse this question; sometimes the child is an only child or for some other reason this question never occurs to it; sometimes the child's first question pertains to some curiosity about its own navel, or "where eggs come from," or "why the hen makes them," or "how they get into the hen," or what is meant by "half shepherd and half St. Bernard." But children do not ask the questions that the books say they ask, and ready-made answers do not always apply.

Whether a child asks the conventional questions or the unexpected questions, and whether it asks questions or not, the parent ought to have some pretty definite notion of when, what, and how to tell a child. A child's questions about the baby should be answered truthfully; all such replies as escape by the stork, cabbage-patch, or grocer-boy route should be avoided. It goes without saying that children's questions should be met seriously and even reverently, and that parents should never speak of nor allude lightly, jokingly, or irreverently to sex relationships in the child's presence.

A child may ask a question prematurely, or at a time when the parent finds it impossible to answer in such a way as to make the desired impression or to avoid the undesirable impression. The postponement should be frankly a postponement, and the parent should answer the question at some later time chosen by the parent and upon the parent's own motion. If the child never affords the parent a natural opening for the first or later conversation, the parent should make the opening by reference to the recent arrival of a baby in the child's home, or in some neighbor's family, or even to the arrival of kittens or chicks.

Such preliminary information should come at or near the first asking of questions, or if no questions are asked, at any convenient time between the ages of six and eight years, and in any case before the child goes to school or mingles much away from home with other children. It is a mistake to suppose that very much need be said to the young child. If the child's normal curiosity is satisfied in a clean way from the right source, that is sufficient. Especially should it be advised of the truth about those facts concerning which it is liable be misinformed in its contacts with other children. Only, parents ought to remember that their child, however carefully brought up and protected, at any time and of its own motion, may itself be that corrupting "other child" against which we are so sedulously warned!

Or, again, the child when it has been duly instructed by parents may without harmful intentions talk too freely with other children. It may do some harm to other children in this; but what is more likely, it may receive harm by calling out uninformed and hurtful conversation from the other side. For this reason, a parent in talking to children should be careful to explain that they should not talk to others. If they are properly brought-up children, their modesty will respond, and their trained obedience will keep faith.

This is the place to try to make clear the importance of such secrecy and confidence between parents and child. There is a secrecy which adds a glamour of pleasurable naughtiness, leading straight to prudery and pruriency with all their consequences. Such secrecy is the sort that develops when parents do take the child into their confidence. Such harmful secrecy is not to be confounded with the confidence between parent and child. In opposing the harmful kind of secrecy, there are those who very wrongly, as I believe, object to any secrecy; who say, "All things are clean; why should any difference whatever be made between the lungs or the stomach, and the sex organs; it is often the very making of any distinction that causes and helps cause all the trouble." Now the case against all secrecy would be valid if the premises of the argument were sound. Roughly speaking, lungs are lungs, and stomachs are stomachs, but the sex organs and their impulses, reflexes, and irradiations are connected with the subtlest complexes of mind and affections, inextricably connected with everything human, with further irradiations into the entire social body.

By all that makes it important to prevent the private and mutual secrecies of children, by so much and ten times more is it important to establish confidential secrecy between parent and child. For in so doing, you not only prevent the undesirable secrecy, but you build normally on modesty; you lay foundations for a true sense of shame, disgust, and disgrace; and in doing so, set up one of the strong defenses against perversions and prurient allurement and seduction.

Prudery should be made impossible and true modesty conserved by proper secrecy in sex matters, and back of that by the proper attitude, conversation, and practice in the child's familiar domestic functions. Prudery and modesty must not be confounded; for by as much as we condemn the one, ought we to value the other.

Up to the time, then, that a child goes to school, everything has probably been done that can be done so far as its instruction is concerned, (1) if the child has been kept as far as possible from foul suggestions from others; (2) if the child has had its questions honestly answered or temporarily though unevasively postponed; (3) if the child knows from its parents' lips that it came into the world from its mother's body, first growing there "beneath its mother's heart" until it was strong enough to be born; and that the mother would never have wished to have her child grow in her body had it not been that there was a strong man who would care for both mother and little child with great love and tenderness; that there has to be a father to love the mother and child, and that, therefore, mother and child must love the father, and the child must love both father and mother, and that this love is what makes the home; and (4) if in the process of imparting information, confidence has been established and modesty conserved.

Anyone who has ever seen a group of six- to ten-year-old boys and girls stand side by side and gaze with rapt but natural wonder and delight at a bureau drawer or chest full of the beautiful little garments waiting and ready for an expected child can never doubt the wisdom of a child's knowing from the start some better version of the story than any of the evasive temporizings of the conventional parent.

What shall the parent do who has never spoken of these things to his child until now the child is ten, eleven, or twelve years of age, and especially if the parent has given the child one of these evasive answers in reply to its innocent questions? It may be said in passing that if the parent has thus evasively answered the child's first questions, he will never be bothered in all probability with any more questions. For the best way to set up the barrier is to answer questions falsely; and one way to establish confidence and to facilitate further communication is to answer truthfully.

The child may know more or less than you think it knows. The parent does not know what a ten- or twelve-year-old child knows or does not know. Again, a parent does not know at what time or in what way or to what extent the child's sexual life and impulse have already awakened. And the parent does not know to what extent the child may know "what ain't so." It is a mistake in most cases for the parent to try to find answers to these questions by questioning the child. For just as a parent may start wrong by deceiving the child, so the child may start wrong by deceiving the parent, and even a pretty good child, especially after it has been deceived by the parent, is likely to follow the same cue when it is questioned by the parent. The parent should not tempt the child to such a misstep.

Again, the parent, whether mother or father, should never try to open the conversation or resume it at a time when the boy or girl is likely to be interrupted or distracted or is eager at the moment to be somewhere else and doing something else. The mother and daughter quietly sewing together, or the father and son off for a walk, or sitting on a log, or lying on the grass, are ready for a confidential talk.

If the boy or girl was deceived in response to its first questions, the father or mother may retract in some such way as this: "Do you remember, Molly, that when you asked me where your baby brother came from, I told you the doctor made us a present? Well, that's the way fathers and mothers answer little children, just as we told you that Christmas presents came from Santa Claus. You came to know that papa and mamma are Santa Claus and that Santa Claus is a fairy story--and so you have probably already learned how the baby came. The baby really grows in the mother's body--did you know that? Do you know how long it takes for it to grow there? No? It takes nine months. Before you were born, you were growing inside of your mother's body. The blood from your mother's body flowed into your body; in this way your body grew. When the baby comes out of its mother's body, it does not hurt the baby, but it hurts the mother. It was so when you were born, but your mother was so happy to think she was to have a baby and to feel it growing inside her body that she did not think much about the pain. If your mother is ever a little tired and cross, you must remember that she loves you beyond anything that pain can measure and that she deserves your tenderest care."

At this or some other fitting time, the father or mother may give the child some further intimation of the process by which the child comes to grow in the mother's body, and in some such way as follows: "Some one may have told you how babies come to grow in their mothers' bodies. But most people are ignorant about these things. I think I can explain it to you a little if you will look for a moment at this flower that I have in my hand, because the coming of a baby in the mother's body is in some ways like the coming of the seed in the body of the flower. You have probably learned at school in your nature-study work that these are--what? Yes, the petals. And these stamens, and this is the pistil. Do you notice the powder on the end of the stamen? That is called pollen. If you put that powder under magnifying glass, each grain will look like a grain of wheat. Now, do you notice that the pistil spreads out here at the base like a vase with a narrow neck and big bowl? I am going to cut the thick part open. Do you notice those tiny things like seeds? Yes, those are seeds, but they would not grow just by themselves. A grain of that pollen gets on to the end of the pistil (sometimes the wind, sometimes a bee puts it there), and immediately it begins to send a long thread from itself right down the center of the pistil, and this thread carries at the front the heart of the pollen grain, and when it reaches the tiny seed the two go together and the heart of the pollen joins with the heart of the seed and then it is a true seed and can grow,--and can grow into another plant that can have flowers that can have seeds, and so on almost forever. No one fully understands this very wonderful fact. We only know that it is a fact,--that the heart of a seed from a father flower had to join to the heart of a seed of a mother flower before a true seed that can grow into a plant is born. And we only know that something like this is true about father and mother animals, and that something like this is true of our own human father and mother."

So much to show how the parent may "break in," for that is often the crucial thing. After the start is made, details may be found in the books provided for just this purpose.[40] Indeed, after beginning, it is sometimes better to put the right book into the boy's hands; or better yet to read the book with the child. Especially is the latter course preferable if the book seems at any point unwise,--and there are few books prepared for children which are not at some point or other unwise. Only, in all this process of definite instruction in which analogies from the life of plants and animals are used, the instructor must make sure that the illustrations are thought of as analogies for the anatomy and biology only, and guards must be reserved, implicitly and explicitly, against the child's supposing that everything in plants and animals is normal for human beings. All that the child learns of reproduction of plants and animals should be related to the home and affectional life even of animals, and the analogy between animals and man should stop far short of that to which in all the animal world there is no real analogy--the life and meaning of the higher order of human family life.

If the proper person to teach the child is the parent and if the parent does not know how, the obvious thing to do is to call the parents together and to try to teach them how. Besides meetings for parents (fathers and mothers together), excellent results have come from meetings for fathers and sons addressed by a man, and from meetings for mothers and daughters addressed by a woman.

The following details as to arrangement and conducting of parents' meetings may be of value. For such meetings in the public school, the consent of the local school board must be obtained. This ought not to be granted if those seeking permission are either cranks or quacks. The Viavi people are said to be obtaining such permission for use of schoolhouses under the specious plea of social hygiene. Others, well intentioned but with extreme purist ideas and unwise methods, occasionally volunteer their services. The school authorities should be cautious. But when those who apply are intelligent and honest and above question as to their standing and judgment, school boards ought not only to consent, but to support and cooperate. A grudging consent, mixed with indifference, finds its way by capillary attraction to the school principals and teachers and constitutes a real hindrance. When the consent of the school authorities has been obtained, the next step is the selection and training of speakers and the notification or the parents. Where permitted, the notices or invitations should be sent out by the school in which the meeting is to be held, by mail, sealed, to every home in the district whence pupils in that school come. This should be done even if the local society has to pay the postage. If the school authorities will not or cannot do this, then cards of invitation should be sent home through the pupils. In either case, the invitation should be so worded as to do no harm to the children who may read it.

Parents' meetings may be addressed by two speakers, a physician and a layman. The two speakers should get to the schoolhouse in time to see that the speaker's desk and chair are not on a high platform too far from the little group of parents. The chair and table should be brought down to the floor close to the seats and the parents brought forward. The principal of the school should introduce the layman, accompanying the physician, to be chairman of the evening. The chairman should make a brief address, as outlined in the syllabus provided by the Committee on Education of the Society, introducing the physician. The physician should make a brief address as outlined in the syllabus, and then, after proper explanations, the physician should resume his chair. Both physician and layman, seated, should engage in a dialogue, in which the layman should endeavor with all the intelligence, sympathy, and skill at his command to put himself in the place of the humblest parent in the room and ask such questions of the physician as such a parent might ask or ought to ask. For example:--

Layman, "Doctor, I have a little boy four years old. When ought I to talk to him about sex matters?"

Physician, "When the child asks questions."

Layman, "What do you mean by that?"

Physician, "Well,--suppose the child asks where the baby came from?"

Layman, "What do you say if the child asks that?"

Physician, "I would tell it that the baby grows in its mother's body," etc.

Layman, "I have a little boy eight years old to whom I have never talked about these things. What do you advise?"

Physician, "I would take the first opportunity, some time when the boy is not likely to be interrupted. Refer to some newly arrived or expected baby and tell him frankly where the baby comes from."

Layman, "But Doctor, I have already told him that a stork brought the baby."

Physician, "Then tell him you told him that as a fairy story like the Santa Claus story, but that now he is old enough to know the truth. Then tell him the truth."

Layman, "But I find it hard to talk about these things and I am afraid my child might ask me questions I could not answer."

Physician, "There are books, a list of which will be handed you, which you can read, and parts or all of which you can read to your child."

Layman, "What if my child asks me a question I can't answer."

Physician, "Don't dodge or evade. If you must postpone an answer, do so frankly with a promise that when you can you will answer, or that you will put him in the way of getting good information by reading or otherwise."

This conversation should be extended to apply to adolescent boys and girls and to young men and women. Enough has been given to show the nature and spirit of the dialogue. The people's interest never flags. The layman must ask all the strategic questions, and he must keep at it until he gets answers in simple, understandable terms. If the physician uses "function" or "coordinate" or "puberty" or "adolescence" or other academic terms, the layman must force simple words at every turn; and in any attempts to describe what a parent should say to a child, the layman should take care that a child's comprehension is reached and that the parent is guided as, to vocabulary. Both speakers should lift the level of their counsels above that of mere physical prudence; they should explain and duly emphasize the moral issue.

Notes:

[40] A classified bibliography is provided at the end of this volume.

CHAPTER IX

TEACHING PHASES: FOR BOYS

By Harry H. Moore

The adolescent boy is the hope of our race. He is the man in the making. Whether he is to be a constructive force, a nonentity, or a destructive force depends largely on influences during this period. In adolescence the processes of destruction are quick and sudden. Statistics of reformatories and prisons show that either crime itself or the moral breakdown which leads to crime begins in boyhood. A study of the lives of great constructive characters shows that their success was largely determined by influences during this period. Certainly, there is no more important task for our nation than the training of our boys.

Adolescence begins at puberty, the transition period during which the sex functions come into full prominence. Its beginning is marked by great physical changes. There are also mental and psychic changes. This fuller development of sex means for the youth new power, new emotion, new capacities for enjoyment of life. At this time the will should emerge as an asset of character. The boy now desires more knowledge of the new world in which he finds himself. He wants to see it by day and by night. He wants to be physically active, or entertained. He belongs to some sort of gang and is loyal to it. His is an age of hero worship.

If the knowledge and the entertainment he finds is wholesome, if the gang is a good one, if the hero is a noble character, if, with emotion and new powers, there is also a strong will, all goes well. But if these influences are not helpful and the will is weak, the result may be quickly disastrous.[41]

Inquiry into the lives of any considerable number of adolescent boys leads one to believe that there exists what almost might be called a conspiracy of silence, misinformation, and bad influence against most boys of this age. Parents for the most part either evade or answer untruthfully the questions of their six-, seven-, and eight-year-old boys regarding birth and reproduction. From this time on, nearly all boys receive many false and low ideas regarding sex, marriage, and the relationship between men and women.

After the stork story, there come incorrect versions of reproduction from boy companions. Then come notes at school, picture cards, comic weeklies, quack advertisements, and unwholesome vaudeville acts. These destructive influences come, for the most part, entirely unsolicited, in response to a normal desire for knowledge and clean entertainment. Boys seldom go to their first shows to see what is vulgar or sensual. They go for clean fun, gymnastics, magicians, and other legitimate amusements. The unwholesome features are thrust upon them.

As a result of these influences on the impressionable mind of the growing boy, he comes to regard sex as low and vile instead of sacred. He acquires a vulgar vocabulary which he necessarily uses in his thinking and sometimes in his conversation. The silence and evasive answers of adults withhold healthful knowledge and increase curiosity. Curiosity often leads to investigation, which often results disastrously.

The specific evil results are of three kinds: (1) masturbation; (2) needless mental suffering due largely to ignorance; (3) illicit intercourse.

Masturbation is prevalent among boys. Two hundred and thirty-two replies were received to a question asked college students regarding their severest temptations of school days. Of these, one hundred and thirty-two said that masturbation had been one of their severest temptations and one hundred and thirty-one said they had yielded to it.[42] Similar inquiries have brought similar results. The sum total of vitality lost to humanity by this practice is great.

There is much needless mental suffering among boys and young men due to ignorance and false ideas advanced by quacks. Groundless fear, brooding anxiety, and despair sometimes start before adolescence and often last into the twenties. Physical peculiarities of no consequence sometimes cause boys to fear that they are abnormal. Unaware of the fact that spontaneous nocturnal emissions are to be expected, many suffer mental anguish. According to one writer, a single New York dealer had 3,000,000 "confidential" letters, "written to advertising medical companies and doctors, mostly by youth with their heart's blood."[43] Large sums of money are obtained by quacks everywhere for treating normal conditions. Many men have applied to the Advisory Department of the Oregon State Board of Health after years of worry. Although those who apply are no longer boys, most of their troubles began in boyhood. A large proportion of the suffering could have been avoided by simple instruction in sexual hygiene.

Social vice often occurs in adolescent boyhood, both as a direct result of unmastered passion and as an indirect result of individual vice. In some cases, the habits a boy forms in his early 'teens make him a subject of venereal disease in later life. A doctor writes, "I am aware that it is popularly supposed that self-abuse and sexual intercourse are antagonistic--by many, the one is regarded as a necessary alternative of the other. So far from being a protective, the former is a most powerful provocative of the latter. According to my own observation, it is not the strongly sexed, the most virile young men, who are most given to licentiousness, but those whose organs have been rendered weak and irritable from this unnatural exercise--in whom the habit of sensual indulgence has been set up, and in whom self-control has not been developed by exercise."[44] This combination of silence, misinformation, and bad influence causes a damnable attitude of mind on the part of the boy toward women, love, marriage, and the home.[45]

The experience of a Chicago business man with his sixteen-year-old son is told in a recent popular magazine. Whether an actual occurrence or not, it is typical of conditions in most any city.

> I do not desire to convey the idea that our boy was a wicked boy. He was not. He was just the average type of what we call the "upper middle-class" boy. He was merely tuned to the low moral tone of the city. Vice to him was not a monster of hideous mien. He had seen it from childhood.... I knew that a greater part of his ideas on patriotism, on women, on the sanctity of marriage were but reflections of views he had heard expressed, often tritely and cleverly, and cynicism born of hearing such things flaunted over the footlights or dished out as "clever" in the newspapers.

In the father's earnest efforts to understand the remedy for the situation, he is reminded of his own experience when he began life in the city. He continues:--

> The boy's words awakened memories. I recalled the sense of shocked and shamed decency I felt when first I came to the city, a boy almost, and fresh from the country; how I tossed in my bed trying to see as right things that every one in the city appeared to accept as a matter of course, but that, from earliest boyhood I had been taught to regard as wicked. I could not for many months become accustomed to seeing immodestly dressed women on or off the stage, or to hearing half-veiled indecency flaunted from the stage, blazoned in the newspapers, or used even in ordinary conversation. I could not get

used to ... scenes and actions directly forbidden as unforgivable at home.[46]

We are horrified by certain vices, the public now and then cries out against specific manifestations of lust, and sometimes it is with difficulty that mobs are restrained from violence But about much of our immorality there is an attractiveness that has made it acceptable and even wins for it applause. The influence is there, and it is insidiously and perniciously working itself into the minds of our boys Many commercialized amusements now exploit the sex impulse. It is impossible to measure the effects of such exploitation.

There are brighter pictures. Those who have intimate relation with hundreds of boys learn to admire the American boy for his earnest desire to be clean and strong and for his attitude toward the sacred things of life. If we give the boy positive help, we may expect him to grow into noble manhood. We would not remove him from all the evil in the world, but we may expect a minimum of harm as a result of contact with evil. We may not expect to keep him away from all foul talk; but we may make foul talk disgust rather than attract him. The American boy is normally clean. If we will do our part, he will respond.

William Holabird represents a type which may well be taken as an example in sex education.

> While chiefly known to the public as a golfer, Holabird was catcher on the school baseball team, half-back on the eleven, held the gold medal for the inter-class track meet, and, in fact, excelled in all athletic sports. As a scholar he always ranked high. He was devotion itself to his parents, his brothers and sisters, respectful to his elders, a leader among his associates, and beloved by all who knew him; tall in stature and muscled like a Greek god, with clear-cut, delicate, refined, and manly features.... With a rare combination of strength

and gentleness accompanied by a bearing and life well illustrating "He was one of nature's noblemen."... A splendid athlete, with a life without a spot or stain, he was a natural leader and a model for all the fellows in the school. The younger boys followed and imitated him.... He hated everything false or unclean or vulgar. To us all, men and boys alike, it was an inspiration to know him.[47]

Our standards for boys and men have been too low. Charles Wagner says, in writing of youth and love:--

Chastity has a host of enemies.... These enemies are quick to throw at your head, as an unanswerable argument, "He who tries to play the angel, plays the fool."

But he continues:--

Many play the fool who have never tried to play the angel. They have not fallen into the mud because they tried to fly too high, but because they began too low down.... A society which permits license in youth, and counsels it, degrades love.... Sin against love at its base,--in youth,--and the life of the whole nation is torn, and suffers immeasurably.... The rule of conduct here is chastity Every infraction is a sin. Though this law may seem difficult and severe, it is the only safe one. Morality without it is but rubbish.[48]

A start has been made. During the last decade, we have declared that we must no longer have two standards of purity, one for the man and another for the woman. We recognize a difference between the nature of the man and the nature of the woman; but as our goal and as our standard for practical life, we have abandoned "the double standard." This is a great advance, for our young people as a whole measure up fairly well to standards which society as a whole sets for them. It is entirely within reason to expect a large majority of our boys to reach full maturity and marriage with an absolutely clean record, as far as personal and social purity are concerned. In fact, we should be constantly working toward a time when the personally impure boy and the socially impure young man will be eliminated. Both the men and the women of our nation must demand this.

There are many ways by which we may guide and help the adolescent. Only the abnormal boy is not active and curious. If we do not provide wholesome activity, boys are likely to find activity which is destructive in its influence. Therefore, we must do far more than mitigate bad influences. We must plan proper regimen. We must supply a steady succession of constructive activities as well as definite instruction to satisfy curiosity. No other course will do.

In the matter of regimen, wholesome food, sufficient sleep, proper clothing, bathing, fresh air, and physical exercise are of great importance. The life and energy and passion of the adolescent boy must not be checked, but diverted into wholesome and constructive channels.

> Excessive mental labor, a sedentary life, pernicious reading, idleness, can transform into a tormenting and persistent desire that which, without it would have been easily mastered. On the other hand, a healthful regimen, energetic habits, amusements and physical fatigue are diversions so useful that, thanks to them, the most critical years pass by unnoticed.[49]

A daily cold shower, followed by a vigorous rubdown, is beneficial if the boy reacts favorably to it. The bath, acts as a sedative.

The value of gymnasium work, track and field athletics, swimming, and "hiking" is constantly demonstrated in the lives of American boys.

> Athletics are to be recommended as possessing a positive prophylactic value against the indulgence of sensual propensities. Physical

exercise serves as an outlet for the superabundant energy which might otherwise be directed toward the sexual sphere. In the period of "storm and stress" which characterizes pubescence and which often leads to nervous perturbation and excitement ... there is no better divertitive from sexual thoughts than active athletic exercises pushed to the point of physical fatigue, as a relief to nerve tension.[50]

In addition, physical exercise tends to develop an ambition to excel, to become physically strong and robust. With such an ambition, boys realize, intuitively to a certain extent, that to succeed they must refrain from vice. Physical exercise has a fourfold moral value: it substitutes wholesome activity for vice; it serves as an outlet for excess of nervous energy; it develops the will; it develops ambition to be virile. All wholesome recreation is an enemy of impurity. Jane Addams says that recreation is stronger than vice, and that recreation alone can stifle the lust for vice.[51] Recreation which involves physical activity is the most helpful to the adolescent boy.

The boy's companions are important. Emerson says, "You send your child to the schoolmaster, but 'tis the schoolboys who educate him."[52] Books which contain high ideals of manhood and also of womanhood are obviously helpful, as are also dramas of this character. And finally those general principles of moral and religious education must be used, without which we can have no strong foundation for clean living.

If we have failed to give proper instruction previous to adolescence, we now have a golden opportunity (and in thousands of cases, our last opportunity) to save the adolescent to a life of purity. As a rule, he has ideas of sex life which are, at least, unwholesome. Curiosity is at a high pitch, and passion is likely to be strong. Nevertheless, the ambitions and ideals of a boy at adolescence are high. He will fight to be clean if he understands that clean living means the acquisition of strength. He would rather have virility than anything else in the world.

As to method, let us deal with the boy as a creature with reason. The best plan is to place before boys a standard of virile manhood, and then to show how such a standard may be met by clean living. Real characters who have achieved high standards of vigor should be shown as heroes worthy of imitation. Lincoln is known by most adolescent boys to have been a man of great physical strength. He was "a man without vices, even in his youth, but full even in ripe age of the sap of virility."[53] The effect of clean living upon nations may also be spoken of. Charles Kingsley writes of the Teuton:[54]--

> It was not the mere muscle of the Teuton which enabled him to crush the decrepit and debauched slave nations.... It had given him more, that purity of his: it had given him, as it may give you, gentlemen, a calm and steady brain, and a free and loyal heart; the energy which comes from self-restraint; and the spirit which shrinks from neither God nor man, and feels it light to die for wife and child, for people and for Queen.

Because thousands of our boys are now growing into manhood who will never receive the advantages of such a plan as we hope will be worked out during the next decade,--boys who are now at the danger point,--an emergency exists that must be met in the best way possible. For these boys, we are now forced to give single talks or short series of talks. Just what facts should be mentioned in a talk to any particular group of boys is a matter which must always be governed by the age, development, and environment of the boys concerned.

The first task for a teacher or a speaker giving a single lesson or a series of lessons is to set up a high standard of manhood. The lessons may concern the development and the conservation of virility. The teacher may explain that virility means not only muscular strength but endurance, energy, will power, and courage; and that in addition to these, a true man has chivalry,--he is concerned for the welfare of others, especially for the safety of women and children. He must possess more than physical prowess; he must possess human virtues or he is no better than a brute. The need for the conservation of virility in the race as well as in the individual should be explained. Boys should see that the conservation of virility in men is of far more importance than the conservation of our water-power or our mines,--that we owe a duty not only to ourselves, but to the nation and to the next generation.

A statement somewhat like the following can then be made: "It is our duty to pass on to the next generation at least a little more vitality than we inherited from the past generation. It is, therefore, important that we understand the main facts of reproduction, so that now we may live right and make no mistakes which may cause us to reproduce inferior children when we mature." The speaker may then describe the wonderful and beautiful process of reproduction in plants, and explain that human reproduction is a similar process.

Under the subject of the development of virility, much time should be spent upon a discussion of various ways by which virility can be developed. The relative values of various kinds of physical exercise, proper eating, the value of fresh air and of sufficient rest should be emphasized. It may then be said that in addition to these things an important source of virility is the absorption of the secretions of various glands by the blood.

The speaker may make a statement similar to this: "When our bodies were designed, we were given reproductive organs for two different and distinct purposes. We have referred to the second and final purpose of reproduction. You already knew more or less about that. The earlier function of the reproductive organs is not understood by most boys. It is this: ***the rebuilding of boys into men***. The first purpose and, in some respects, the most important purpose of the reproductive organs is to rebuild a boy into a man. It would be absolutely impossible for us to become men were it not for these organs. I will explain this by three illustrations."

These three illustrations are generally very effective: an explanation of the influence of the thyroid gland upon development; a comparison of two horses, one of which was castrated when a colt; and the effect of castration upon boys in Oriental countries.

The speaker may then say that the testicles do two things: first, manufacture the male germ cells, spermatozoa, which are the most highly potentialized and highly energized portions of matter in all living nature; and, second, secrete a substance that is absorbed by the blood, giving tone to the muscle, power to the brain and strength to the nerves. It should be made clear that this is one of the great sources of virility. From the illustrations referred to, a boy is likely to draw conclusions regarding the vital importance of the functions of the testicles and regarding any possible misuse of them. It may be well at this point to use a cross-section drawing showing the scrotum, the testicle, the seminal vesicle, and the bladder.[55] Some teachers will consider it desirable to add that some boys, who do not understand the high purposes of these organs, misuse them; that when such boys realize their mistake, if they stop absolutely and at once, nature comes to the rescue and restores virility.

The talks should be essentially constructive. To warn boys against horrible effects of masturbation and to tell them things not to do is a poor method. It is far better to explain that by keeping clean a boy may acquire virility. The boy can draw conclusions.

In referring to the normality of seminal emissions, it should be explained that the fluid excreted by a nocturnal seminal emission comes from the seminal vesicles up in the body. This will show that the loss of fluid involved in a nocturnal emission is different from the loss caused by masturbation.[56] In this connection, boys should be warned against quack doctors; also against their advertisements which are often worded to scare the ignorant.

The venereal diseases should be referred to in talks to adolescent boys. In this connection, the four sex lies may be vigorously contradicted. These are (1) that gonorrhea is no worse than a bad cold; (2) that sexual intercourse is necessary for the preservation of health; (3) that emissions are dangerous and lead to debility, lost manhood, and insanity; and (4) that one standard of morality is right for men and another for women.

It should be explained that although both animals and human beings are endowed with the sex instinct, only human beings have the gift of control. That the sex instinct is a great blessing, and not a curse, should be made clear. It may be stated that various blessings are sometimes converted into sources of destruction when not controlled. A spirited horse is a source of great enjoyment, but if not controlled may maim us for life. Fire is a great blessing and a great joy to us when we are camping by a lake or in the mountains; but, beyond our control, it may cause forest fires. Temper, the capacity for anger, is highly desirable; but it must be controlled or murder may result. We must control the sex instinct, or it may control us and sink us lower than the brutes. On the other hand, if we control this instinct, we gain virility, a keener appreciation of the beauties of life, and life itself becomes richer and fuller.

In conclusion, the appeal should be for clean living for the sake of physical strength and vigor, not for one's own sake, but for the sake of country and future wife and children.

The standard toward which we are working in sex education involves the dissemination throughout the school curriculum of such information as we now give in a single talk. In addition to such nature-study work and simple biology and physiology and hygiene as should be included in the lower grades, there should be instruction in biology and in personal hygiene required for all upper-grammar and all high-school students, as soon as well qualified teachers are available. In personal hygiene a proper amount of sex hygiene should be incorporated; and with the treatment of other diseases, gonorrhea and syphilis should be given adequate attention; the idea of the whole plan being to place all these matters in their proper setting, without undue emphasis on matters of sex.

Either (first) as a part of one of these courses or (second) as a part of some other general course, or (third) as a separate course, the following subjects should be considered:--

1. What is virility?
  (a) Virility and the next generation.
  (b) Virility and our nation.
  (c) Types of virility.

2. Muscle, exercise, and virility.
  (a) How, when, and where to exercise.
  (b) "Second wind."
  (c) Rest.
  (d) Will power.

3. Food, good blood, and virility.
  (a) What to eat.
  (b) Tobacco.
  (c) Clogged-up machines.
  (d) Blood and other body fluids.

4. Fresh air, bathing, and virility.
  (a) Sleeping-porches, camping.

(b) How to bathe.

(c) Change of clothes.

5. Virility and disease.
  (a) Disease generally an unnecessary evil.
  (b) Relative seriousness of tuberculosis, typhoid, syphilis, gonorrhea, diphtheria, colds, headaches, adenoids, enlarged tonsils.
  (c) Body and mind.

6. Virility and certain glands.
  (a) Importance of the thyroid gland and the testicles.
  (b) Difference between stallion and gelding.
  (c) Seminal vesicles.
  (d) Quack doctors.

7. Virility and reproduction.

8. Fatherhood and the next generation.

In our attitude toward the boy, we must show him that we respect him, that we have faith and confidence in him, and expect great things of him. We should meet him on the level of a boy's everyday interests in sport, use simple language, and no unnecessary technical terms. Some workers with boys unwisely force confessions of guilt. We should respect the boy's right of privacy.

When we deal with boys in the mass, the grouping is difficult. Boys who have reached the period of puberty should be in a separate group from pre-pubescents, and boys who are well advanced in adolescence--those who have been pubescent for two or three years--should be taught in still a third group. This applies to single talks as well as to courses of instruction.

As far as we know the best basis of division between the pubescent and pre-pubescent boy (when physical examinations are not possible) is the change of voice. Only one who understands these matters well and knows the boys should do the grouping. Even such a man should not adopt an arbitrary basis of grouping but must take one boy at a time and place him in the group for which he seems best fitted.

We should endeavor to include the father in our plans of sex instruction and be careful not to break down such confidence as exists between father and son. We shall find that only a small proportion of fathers give their sons any instruction in sexual matters, and that it is difficult to stir them to action. In one investigation, it was found that one hundred boys out of one hundred and twenty-one had received no sex instruction from their fathers.[57]

When confidence between father and son does exist, we should help the father rather than relieve him of his task. It is difficult to discover fathers who have confidential relations with their boys unless each family is dealt with separately. The Oregon Social Hygiene Society has conducted father and son meetings, and has required the father either to accompany the boy or sign a card signifying his willingness to have his son attend. Few fathers have attended, sometimes none at all. On one occasion there were thirty-five boys and not one father.[58] Requiring permission may be regarded as an assumption that the talk is questionable; and, furthermore, the requiring of special permission is likely to create an undesirable attitude on the part of the boy. Plans for father and son meetings which will be free from these objections will possibly be developed by other schools or social hygiene societies. Our aim is so to educate one generation of boys that when they become fathers they will inform their son regarding these sacred relationships and functions of life.

     *   *   *   *   *

The boy is normally clean and wholesome. His first question regarding the origin of life is a good question. When denied wholesome information, the further investigation which often follows is indicative of desirable qualities of character. Later, though disturbed by false ideas which have been forced upon him, he still wishes to be clean and strong. He desires to master low passions. He would rather have muscular strength and endurance and energy and will power and courage and chivalry than any amount of money. He shudders at the thought of causing suffering to an innocent woman or child. He would sacrifice his life for the girl whom he regards as the personification of loveliness and purity. If we will but deal with him fairly and honestly, he will see in birth an ever-recurring miracle; he will regard his body as a sacred temple; he will see in sex power a source of richer and fuller life; he will respect women; he will regard marriage as the most sacred relationship in life. Thus noble manhood, a nation's greatest asset, will in large measure be achieved.

Notes:

[41] John L. Alexander (editor), **Boy Training.** Association Press, New York, especially pp. 11 to 22.

[42] **Pedagogical Seminary**, vol. IX, no. 3. Worcester, Massachusetts.

[43] G. Stanley Hall, **Adolescence**, vol. I, p. 459.

[44] Prince A. Morrow in the **Transactions** (vol. I, p. 88) of the American Society of Sanitary and Moral Prophylaxis.

[45] Charles Wagner, **The Simple Life**, p. 181. (McClure, Phillips & Co.) Caleb Williams Saleeby, **Parenthood and Race Culture.** (Moffat, Yard & Co.) Francis G. Peabody, **Jesus Christ and the Social Question**, p. 162. (Grosset & Dunlap.)

[46] "What my Boy Knows," *American Magazine*, New York, April, 1913.

[47] Robert E. Speer, *Young Men Who Overcame*, p. 21. (Fleming H. Revell Co., Chicago.)

[48] Charles Wagner, *Youth*, pp. 248-50.

[49] Charles Wagner, *Youth*, p. 246.

[50] *The Boy Problem*, Educational Pamphlet no. 4, p. 26, of the American Society of Sanitary and Moral Prophylaxis, 105 West 40th Street, New York.

[51] Jane Addams, *The Spirit of Youth and the City Streets*, p. 20. The Macmillan Company, New York.

[52] Emerson, *Education*, p. 38. Riverside Monograph Series.

[53] Henry Bryan Binns, *Abraham Lincoln*, p. 356.

[54] Charles Kingsley, *The Roman and the Teuton*, p. 46.

[55] Winfield S. Hall, M.D., *From Youth into Manhood*, p. 32. Association Press, New York.

[56] Hall, *Reproduction and Sexual Hygiene.*

[57] From an investigation conducted by Dr. Winfield S. Hall.

[58] "A Social Emergency," First Annual Report of the Social Hygiene Society of Portland, Oregon, and the Bulletin of the Oregon Social Hygiene Society, vol. I, no. I.

CHAPTER X

TEACHING PHASES: FOR GIRLS

By Bertha Stuart

The normality of the reaction to sex knowledge depends upon the physical and mental training of the child. Our thoughts concerning girls run in fixed grooves. We believe that, in babyhood, instinct leads them to prefer dolls to their brothers' guns and a little later renders them less active physically and more gentle and tractable mentally. Because of this supposed difference in instincts and because of a well-defined picture in our own minds of the final product we wish to evolve, we build a structure externally fair, but lacking the foundation to enable it to resist the stress of time and circumstance. Because of our traditionally different ways of dealing with girls and boys, we have produced girls who are not healthy little animals, but women in miniature with nervous systems too unstable to cope successfully with the strain of our modern complex life.

The stability of the nervous system is dependent upon the proper development of the fundamental centers. Incomplete development of the lower parts means incomplete development in the higher. These fundamental centers are stimulated to growth and development especially by the activity of the large muscle masses. Not only is the development of the brain and nervous system dependent upon muscular activity, but the growth and activity of the vital organs as well,--the heart, lungs, and digestive system,--and the normality of sex life.

All this we acknowledge in the case of the boy. Even with him, we fail to live up to our convictions, as is shown by the long hours of inactivity in school and the lack of suitable activities during recess periods. But on the whole we encourage the boy to run and climb and jump and take distinct pride in these accomplishments.

The same accomplishments in our girls occasion alarm; we have an ideal of gentle womanhood. Even though unrestrained up to the time she attends school, the girl then enters upon the long career of physical repression which characterizes her training. Parents, teachers, neighbors, and schoolmates often seem to conspire to curb all the natural impulses upon which her health and rounded development depend.

Aside from the reproductive organs, the physical mechanism of the girl is much like that of the boy. There is no peculiarity in the structure of the reproductive organs to prohibit vigorous activity. The development and health of these organs and their ligamentous supports are dependent primarily upon the quality and free circulation of the blood, both of which are preeminently the result of fresh air and exercise. If the muscular system in general is well developed, there is no reason why the muscular and ligamentous structure of the reproductive organs should not be equally well developed. To insure their proper development, exercise is essential.

A questionnaire answered by girls at the University of Oregon shows that, with few exceptions, plays and games were not indulged in throughout the high-school period and systematic playing ceased for the majority in the seventh and eighth grades. This custom prevails throughout the country. Just at the time when a girl needs abundant and free open-air play to develop the muscles, train endurance of the heart, and increase the capacity of the lungs, she omits it altogether. This is one of the chief factors in the anaemias and poor circulation common in that period. The derangement in the blood results in digestive disturbances and loss of appetite, followed by headache and lassitude which further disincline the girl for activity. Add to this the nervous strain incident to endeavors to carry on a successful social career, the nerve tension resulting from the unhygienic clothing assumed at this time, the lack of the steadying influence of home responsibilities, and we have ample cause for the nervous, high-strung girl who is becoming so common that we are in danger of regarding her as the normal girl.

So greatly has the school curriculum encroached upon the home that the girl has no longer time to share its responsibilities, nor is there longer time for the family reading-circle, or music, or games for the maintenance of the unity and fellowship of the home. This condition cannot but react unfavorably upon the nervous system. If the brain is not rested and the emotions satisfied by the relationships in the home, a feverish unrest, a nervous irritability, a futile search supplant the calmness of spirit, stableness of reactions and depth of contentment which must be long continued to become a habit of mind.

Our school systems of to-day are designed for a girl as strong physically as a boy; in fact stronger than most of our city boys. Our girls should possess as much vitality as our boys; but until we change our methods of dealing with girls, we must treat them as they exist and not as the normal individuals we hope some day to evolve. Most girls have disorders,--"nervousness," headache, backache, constipation, colds, fatigue, or pain at the menstrual period. So common are these disturbances that we consult a physician only in extreme cases, and rarely seek the cause of the condition or attempt more than temporary relief. A pain which under ordinary circumstances would receive medical attention is viewed with resignation when coincident with the menses. As a consequence of this neglect, many girls suffer unnecessary drains upon their vitality.

We find all degrees of menstrual pain. It may be so mild as to be little more than discomfort, or so intense that unconsciousness results. The pain may be sharp and knife-like, or it may be a dull ache. It may be localized, low down in one or both sides, distributed over the whole abdomen or concentrated in the back. With this pain, there may be headache, or a headache may be the only symptom. Frequently there is gastro-intestinal disturbance--nausea, vomiting, diarrhoea, or constipation. In anaemic cases fainting is common.

Local or operative treatment is not as a rule necessary, for the majority of cases yield to a strict regime of hygienic living. The regime should include regulation of sleeping, of eating, of hours of work and relaxation, of dressing and of exercise. The exercise should be prescribed and directed by a person trained in medical gymnastics.

Frequently mental disturbances are associated with the phenomenon of menstruation. The most usual symptoms are heightened irritability, hysterical manifestations and depression. Depression is often the only symptom; to some girls the premonitory "blues" signify the approach of the period. Occasionally we encounter the reverse, an excessive stimulation and feeling of well-being and strength. There is some loss in the power of concentration. In normal cases, however, this loss is less than many people suppose it to be. Lassitude and a feeling of general debility are confined chiefly to the anaemic cases.

The mental symptoms clear up as the physical condition is improved, aided by a sensible attitude toward the whole process. Often girls who suffer some pain live through the whole month in dread of the period. This attitude should be changed, by lessening the pain and by psychic therapy. Psychic therapy has proved successful in obstinate cases.

The girl who suffers considerably from any of these disorders at the monthly period should be relieved from the strain of examinations, the classroom, and lessons which must be learned, although mental hygiene requires that her mind be kept active and her interests in quiet pleasures stimulated. She should not be left to introspection and morbidness or to the sickly sentimental thoughts often recommended for her. This alone would cause her to exhibit some of the so-called "phenomena" of adolescence. Many of these phenomena are abnormal and are traceable to low physical vitality and lack of strong mental interests. The menstrual period should not be attended by pain or discomfort; nor should our girls be brought up to regard it as a time of sickness. When our girls are taught that normal girls experience no indisposition at this time, they will not be resigned to pain. The high-school life of the girl below the average in physical vitality cannot be regulated to her advantage in a co-educational school. Cities should maintain girls' high schools, taught by women teachers, for all girls upon whom the stress and strain of competition with normal individuals would react unfavorably. In the majority of cases, menstrual pain in girls is due to nerve tension, anaemia and poor circulation, improper clothing, and mental attitude. The girls who experience no pain are those who have led an active out-of-door life and have never stopped playing.

The character and arrangement of a girl's clothing is one of the most important matters in her whole regimen. Clothing may neutralize the beneficial effects of her otherwise hygienic habits. The long-continued even though light pressure of the corset--and it is seldom light--interferes with the free circulation of the blood. The alteration in intro-abdominal pressure is conducive to misplacements of abdominal and pelvic organs; the anterior pressure on the iliac bones, the result of the modern long hip corset, is a fruitful source of partial separation of sacro-iliac joints--the cause of many backaches. Respiration is limited, the free play of abdominal muscles is prevented, constipation is promoted, and digestion is impaired. The strain on muscles and nerves caused by high-heeled shoes is a prolific source of headache and backache and reduced efficiency. Women have no conception how greatly their susceptibility to fatigue is increased and their total efficiency reduced by their methods of dress. The pity is that the majority will not learn unless the decrees of fashion change.

The hygienic problems of girls in industry will largely disappear when it becomes a matter of common knowledge that industrial efficiency is dependent upon physical efficiency. The physical efficiency of the worker cannot be maintained at its highest standard when the period allotted to rest is too short to allow the body to rebuild its tissues and dispose of the toxic products of fatigue. All activity must be balanced by rest. If this equilibrium between expenditure and income is disturbed, exhaustion ensues. If long continued, it results in permanent impairment of health. The organism poisoned by its own toxic products is incapable of productive effort and the output will steadily diminish as the fatigue increases. The present long working day causes a progressive diminution in the vitality of the worker, defeats its own end, and leaves the girl weak in the face of temptations.

The housing of unmarried girls is a very serious question. Homes for working-girls require skillful management and a matron of insight and sympathy. The bedrooms may be small, but well lighted and ventilated. There should be a sunny dining-room, a library, several small parlors, attractively furnished, a gymnasium which could be used for dancing, shower baths, and an assembly room for concerts, lectures, and moving pictures. This should be in charge of a trained social leader who would direct entertainments and stimulate wholesome interests. With an establishment of this kind we should not find so many of our girls on the streets or seeking diversion in cheap theaters and dance halls. When girls are able to live,--not simply exist in the deadening monotony of alternation between work and sleep,--their heightened mental activity, interest, and enthusiasm will prove a valuable asset to employers.

One of the chief requisites of the mental training of girls is a knowledge, supplied at the right time and in the right way, of the fundamental principles of reproduction. With such knowledge the girl's mind will not be distracted by curiosity, or become morbid, when, instead of intelligent response, the girl meets with evasions and attempted concealments. She should not receive this knowledge in the form of isolated facts, but as a correlated part of a great whole to be assimilated gradually. The girl who is trained in this way will understand and accept human reproduction as a natural process.

Questionnaires show that a majority of girls hear the facts of reproduction at the age of seven or eight, a few younger, and a few at the age of ten,--almost none at a later age. The majority hear these facts from children a year or two older, a few from their mothers, and the rest from books. A large number experience a feeling of disgust which remains with them until they receive better information. Their questions disclose a depth of ignorance and misconception which is appalling.

Girls, at the age of twelve, thirteen, or fourteen, should have presented to them a course in physiology which includes the anatomy and hygiene of the reproductive organs. This is carefully omitted from present-day secondary-school textbooks. This course should use charts, pictures, and models. The significance of menstruation, the hygiene of the period, and the causes and prevention of pain should be explained. Under the hygiene of the period, the daily bath should be urged, with caution against chills, in which lies the only possibility of injury. The fertilization of the ovum and cell division may be described by use of the blackboard and embryological models of the later stages of development. The forces which bring about labor can be explained without unduly stressing the attending pain.

The course would be incomplete without a discussion of the necessity of careful selection in marriage from the eugenic standpoint. The perils and results of the venereal diseases should be told simply and frankly. The instruction in eugenics, like that in reproduction, should be progressive and indirect, at least up to the age of seventeen or eighteen years. Again it may be correlated with plant life by pointing out the beauty of strong, hardy plants and their relation to the seeds. Children can be taught to save the seeds of the most beautiful blossoms for the following year. Instruction can be continued with the lower animals. The child will then grow up with the idea that strength and vigor and freedom from disease are desirable qualities, and must exist in the parent if they are to exist in the offspring. The idea can be readily carried over to the human family. At the age of seventeen or eighteen, the influence of heredity and the effects of the racial poisons should be fully explained, and emphasis laid upon qualities necessary for racial betterment.

For our girls the first need is a sounder physical organism, which can be attained only through the systematic continuance of physical activities through childhood and girlhood; the second need is sounder mental interests, which can be attained only through the systematic guidance of the mental activities throughout childhood and girlhood; and the third need is instruction in laws of reproduction.

CHAPTER XI

MORAL AND RELIGIOUS PHASES

By Norman Frank Coleman

Personal and social hygiene in matters of sex are, in very important ways, dependent upon moral and religious training. On the other hand, morals and religion are in important ways dependent upon forces set free by the growth and activity of sex instincts and powers. One of the most significant facts in modern social progress is its recognition of this interdependence of mind and body. We have learned that physical health depends upon peace of mind, hopefulness, courage, and many other things that have seemed in the past to be purely mental or spiritual; and we have learned also that the character of people and the spirit in which they do their work depend upon their health, upon conditions of food and warmth and shelter, things which in the past have been regarded as affecting only the physical man. It is now somewhat out of date to set physical conditions over against moral and religious; every great human problem is more and more clearly seen in this day to involve all these conditions in its rise, and to require thoughtful consideration of them all for its solution. As we face the problems of sex, we must recognize the importance of fresh air, exercise, wholesome food, clean cups and clean towels, and we must also recognize the importance of clean thoughts and high purposes. We must know clearly the facts of biological and medical science, and with them in mind we must touch the springs of conduct in affection and imagination. Our aim must be to achieve that mastery over the forces of life finely expressed by Browning's Rabbi ben Ezra: "Nor soul helps flesh more, now, than flesh helps soul."

We may consider, first, how, in matters of sex, flesh helps soul; second, how soul helps flesh; and third, how in normal childhood and youth soul and flesh grow together in mutual help.

The first great outstanding fact is that the physical powers of sex reach maturity in the same years in which the moral and religious instincts are greatly quickened. If we recall our youth, we must realize that, in the years between twelve and twenty, our lives were greatly disturbed and perplexed, and also greatly exalted and inspired by desires and impulses partly toward the opposite sex and partly toward the service of God and our fellows. In the normal adolescent boy or girl there is a powerful expanding and enriching of sex thoughts and desires and purposes. There is also a rapid development of social sympathy and passion; the revolutionary movements of all lands are recruited from those who like Shelley have in their youth vowed,--

> "I will be wise,
> And just, and free, and mild, if in me lies
> Such power, for I grow weary to behold
> The selfish and the strong still tyrannize
> Without reproach or check."

And there is a wonderful flowering of the young life in religious feeling and aspiration; a large majority of religious conversions take place in adolescence.

We can scarcely escape the conviction that these are not different awakenings, but rather different phases of the one great awakening of the young life as it prepares for the tasks and responsibilities of manhood and womanhood. The part that sex development plays in this awakening has been variously stressed by different special students of the physiology and psychology of adolescence. Some scientists have not hesitated to give it first place and to treat social passion and religious enthusiasm as secondary manifestations of sex energy.[59] However that may be, we know that each speaks naturally in terms of the other. The religious mystic of the Middle Ages was devoted to the Divine Lover or the Heavenly Lady, and the modern revolutionary is *wedded* to the Cause. On the other hand, the lover naturally adopts the language of religion to express his devotion to the lady of his heart. The water-tight compartment theory of life is in these days thoroughly discredited. We know that the various powers of soul and body are related and interdependent, and we feel sure that the developing powers of sex do have very vital relation to developing powers of moral purpose and religious aspiration. In support of this relation we recall the unfortunate effects upon the character of those who by chance or the barbarity of men have been desexed in childhood. We must allow for other factors at work here, yet the clearly established facts of the stunting of mental and moral growth in desexed children reinforce our own experience and observation, and indicate that the energies that are developed with sex and maturity are largely available for moral and religious growth. The youth with full sex consciousness and impulse is normally the youth of abundant energy for moral and religious activity. It seems, therefore, quite fundamental to the right understanding of sex that we consider the body, not the enemy of the soul, but its friend; not a clog upon the spiritual growth of boy and girl advancing into manhood and womanhood, but an important source of energy for the upward climb.

When we turn to the second part of our discussion and ask how in matters of sex soul helps flesh, the need and the fact are clearer and perhaps more urgent. Dante found the souls of the lustful in the second circle of hell, driven hither and thither by warring winds,--

> "The stormy blast of hell
> With restless fury drives the spirits on,
> Whirled round and dashed amain with sore annoy."

Here we have clear recognition of the two great characters of sex impulse, its violence and its fitfulness. In the one character it needs to be subdued that it may not destroy; in the other it needs to be directed that it may build up.

As we look back through history, and as we look abroad through our land and through all civilized lands, one of the most conspicuous facts concerning the powers of sex is their frightful destructiveness. The spectacle of wasted manhood and womanhood, of depleted powers in body, mind, and soul, is in history and in present society appalling. It is so oppressive that it has driven many thoughtful men and women to despair. Men otherwise hopeful and purposeful here become gloomy and fatalistic; they have no hope that lust will ever be effectively controlled.

Such pessimism, however, contradicts the history as well as the instincts of the race. In the face of great evils there have always been those who would sit down in discouragement despair; every great destructive force in human history has daunted some men to the point of inactivity. Yet the evils have been controlled. Ignorant and fearful people have said, "This thing is beyond human power; it is useless for us to struggle against fate." Yet men of vision and of courage have struggled and won. No man of moral passion and religious purpose can adopt an attitude of passive submission to the forces of destruction. We can admit no necessary evil, or the battle of human progress is lost. We ask ourselves soberly, therefore, how this tremendous outrush of destructive energy may be controlled. The answer is plain. Men have by the agency of fire itself constructed the means by which fire is controlled and domesticated; they have turned disease against itself, and by the agency of antitoxins have conquered it; they are learning to arouse and organize the fighting spirit of men against its own most ancient and fearful expression and are enlisting soldiers of peace in a war against war. Even so the race depends upon the higher affections for control of the lower, and lust is controlled by love. I talked once to a young man in college who had given himself to sexual vice when he had been in high school; until a year before I spoke with him, he had supposed that virtually all men were and must be sexually indulgent. For twelve months he had kept himself clean. I inquired why and how. He replied simply that he had fallen in love with a young woman and wished to marry her. His former course now seemed to him shameful and unmanly. Lust yielding to love! In one of his sonnets to the woman who afterward became his wife, Edmund Spenser says:--

> "You frame my thoughts and fashion me within:
> You stop my tongue and teach my heart to speak:
> You calm the storm that passion did begin:
> Strong through your cause, but by your virtue weak."

In our own experience, as far as we have achieved victory in our own bodies and minds over our baser passions, we have achieved it by the power of the higher affections. It is a fact of common experience that love calms the storm that passion did begin. So Spenser's lady strengthened passion by her charm, but weakened it by her virtue.

Nor is this the only higher affection that, in the practical experience of men, has controlled and transformed animal passion. Thousands of fully sexed men have, through the centuries, turned their bodily and mental energies so fully to devoted service for God and their fellows as to rise above the clamoring demands of physical appetite, in the vigorous terms of the New Testament making themselves eunuchs for the kingdom of God's sake. This is a hard saying, and the experience it treats of must always be confined to a small number of men; yet it goes far toward demonstrating a general possibility, and it should effectively dispose of the "necessity" argument, by which men often excuse their vicious practices.

One thing more should be said on this subject of control. Not only are the higher, more spiritual affections the most effective masters of the lower; they are the *only* effective masters. Public reprobation can do much, but it is ineffectual with large numbers of relatively unattached members of society, and it is impotent against secret vice. Motives of cautious fear are always weak with full-blooded and generous youth, and they are likely to become weaker with all men as medical science discovers ways to prevent or escape the most obviously fearful consequences of sexual license.

A familiar phrase comes to my mind, as no doubt it comes to yours: "The expulsive power of the higher affections"; yet I think that phrase is not quite suitable. It is not a question of expulsion. It is not wholly a question of control; it is mainly a question of direction. What we need to-day with boys and girls for the solving of the sex problems is to direct those energies, which in their false direction are destructive, into right and healthful ways; that is, we need to socialize and elevate that affection, which in baser forms has aspects of ugly animalism.

As one of the solutions of the problem of control it has been proposed to separate the sexes in the adolescent years. From my point of view, this would defeat our object. In the association of boys and girls during the adolescent period, we may enlist the higher affections for the control and the direction of the powers that are set free by sex impulses developed in that very period of life.

What happens in the experience of the normal boy? In this period of early adolescence he finds within himself a wonderful quickening of mind,--impulses, feelings, longings that he does not understand. These impulses, feelings, longings, perplex him, it may be for years. They reach out vaguely, blindly toward the opposite sex, sometimes in a perverted way, but oftener naturally and honestly. Then the young man falls in love. At once his more or less vague, cloudy, incoherent, formless feelings and purposes are concentrated, directed, and fixed in devotion to a young woman whom he idealizes, almost deifies. That is the first stage in the natural directing and forming of sex powers and impulses toward social, moral, and religious ends. Of course the young man may discover, after a while, that the first object of his fancy is not so angelic as he thought. By and by his fancy changes and may rove to several other maidens before he reaches maturity; but each successive experience, if he is true to his better self, concentrates his affections and directs them, until, if he is fortunate, in the course of time he finds his true mate and enters upon marriage. He is now fairly equipped for what most of us know to be a long course in the discipline of the selfish, the personal, the more or less brute desires and ambitions of man. Here he learns to subject himself, his own comfort, his own ends, his own ambitions, to the good of his wife and her happiness, to the good of his children and the satisfaction of their needs. Then, more and more, after having concentrated the powers of his spirit through faithful courtship and through happy marriage and fatherhood, the man is able to diffuse these same energies through many channels, for the protection of all sorts and conditions of women and children. The man is now a citizen, a member of society, with developed powers of social sympathy, of social energy. How has he developed these powers? Not by any supposition that the early sex instincts he felt in his boyhood were wholly animal and must be atrophied by disuse, but by gathering and directing them into the right channels. Direction, like control, depends upon enlightened, purposeful, persistent love.

In the third place, we may consider how, in matters of sex, the flesh and the soul may grow together in mutual help. The essential facts and the vital importance of the sex life appeal to the developing boy or girl in four great relations, in relation to father and mother, in relation to the strength and grace of his or her own body and mind, in relation to his or her future family, and in relation to society in general. These appeals come in successive periods and open the way to healthful instruction and guidance from childhood up to manhood and womanhood.

Sex questions first arise in the child's mind in connection with parenthood. The first thing a little boy or girl needs to know is that the young life is sheltered and fed during long months in the mother's body, and that the father had a share in that life. Is it not amazing that in this twentieth century we find many girls twelve years old and over who do not know that their father had any share in starting their lives? I knew of a girl nineteen years old, a student in college, who did not know that a man had any essential part in bringing children into the world, but supposed, when any question of illegitimate childbirth was raised, that possibly God punished a bad woman by sending her a baby before she was married. It is little short of criminal that many girls are allowed to reach adolescence with no sex thought or image clearly in their minds except such as they have received directly or indirectly from animals. If boys and girls knew from the beginning that a part of the father's life and a part of the mother's life united to form the beginning of their lives, the question of sex would begin on a plane where there were religious, moral, and spiritual associations, and an atmosphere of love and holiness. These young people could then see the facts of sex clearly instead of through the mists of prurient fancy and suggestion as they see them now.[60] The boy and girl who know these two tremendous facts of the nurturing care of the mother before birth, and the cooperation of the father and mother in the beginning of life, are fortified against the principal moral and spiritual dangers that they are to face in the future.

The next information and guidance needed by our boys and girls concerns the influence of sex upon their own development. The objection is continually raised that it is not well for little children to have sex thoughts emphasized in their minds. But at present no boy or girl grows up and plays among other children, or hears talk on the streets, or goes to work in factory or store, without hearing these facts emphasized day by day, emphasized unhealthily and distorted shamefully. We propose simply to have the emphasis shifted and lightened for it will be lightened if the facts are given truly and in right relations. Boys and girls should learn, at the same time they are learning facts of nutrition, excretion, respiration, and circulation of the blood, those facts regarding sex which are most important for healthy growth of mind and body. They should know that the organs of reproduction have a definite relation to the natural and healthful development of the full powers of their bodies in future years; that internal secretions of these organs coming into the blood help to build up bones and muscles, help to make their nerve fibers active and vigorous, help to form their brains, and help to equip them for manly strength and womanly grace in the years that are to come. These are very simple matters. These facts of sex can be conveyed by just a few sentences of clear, considerate, wise information at the right time, in relation to the other facts of bodily development.

Considering now the period of puberty, we find additional needs, for no boy or girl reaches puberty, under ordinary conditions, without knowing that it brings the possibility of fatherhood and motherhood, brings the possibility of that process that we call fertilization, in which the life of plants and animals begins. The boy or girl who reaches this age has a right to know what fertilization means, and what fertilization implies; has a right to the simple biological facts which will tell him the relation between the life of the parents and the life of the child, the mysterious relation in body and mind that we call heredity. The beginning of the socializing of sex energy and sex power depends upon recognition of the fact that this power that develops in the young man and young woman at puberty is not to be used for selfish gratification, is not primarily a source of pleasure, but has a very direct relation to the health, intelligence, and happiness of others. This relation may be enforced by a simple study of succeeding generations of flowers and the ways in which forms, colors, and sizes originate and are handed down from generation to generation in wonderful variety. Or it may be illustrated from an observation of the beginnings of sex in infusoria; how tiny animals in stagnant water grow to full size and each divides simply into two to form a new generation; how this simple asexual process continuing for several generations results in growing weakness and old age, steadily decreasing size, steadily decreasing vitality until there comes a time when one infusorian unites with another. There sex begins. That union of two individuals is required to restore youth, to refresh vitality and energy, and to produce greater variety in the forms of life. When a boy or girl knows these simple facts, he is better able to understand the power of reproduction than he can possibly be if they are not before him, or if all he has heard has been ceaseless reiteration of the pleasures of selfish indulgence of sex appetite.

Finally, when the boy and the girl come into later adolescence and face manhood and womanhood, they are ready to know some of the larger social aspects of sex. They are ready to know of the diseases brought on by perverted sex habits; of the frightful waste of those who give themselves to licentiousness, the frightful waste of strength and youthful energy not only in those that actually go down, but in those that survive. More than that, seeking right relations of themselves to society, they need to know the social aspects of sex. The young man needs to know what it means for a woman to bear a child; he needs to know the social and economic dependence of the pregnant woman and of the young mother, so that he may realize what the power of fatherhood means in the actual work of society. I cannot imagine any man talking glibly of the necessary evil, or of man's inability to control sex passions, if he knows the social facts of sex. Any young man who knows even a part of the burden his mother bore for him, if he has a spark of manhood in his being, is surely fortified against temptation to selfish indulgence. If, beyond that, he can see the relation of the home to society, the relative steadiness and dependability of a worker with a wife and children, who bears the home burdens in a man's way, as compared with the floating, homeless wanderer who walks our streets; if he knows these central facts and the dependence of the home upon the faithfulness of the man and the presence of the man, if he has a spark of patriotism in his heart, he must realize in his thought and in his practice the necessity for the socialization of that passion which, though it begin in individual and selfish forms, issues in such fateful social consequences.

The solution of this great, urgent, pressing problem, which we are feeling the weight of more and more in these years of careful investigation of our social conditions, will come in frankly recognizing the beginnings upon which the whole sex life in mind and body is based, and in transforming fundamentally important animal instincts and desires into higher affections, humanizing them for the sake of the loved one, for the sake of family, for the sake of the social brotherhood and sisterhood in which we are members.

My closing word is one which seems to me most significant of the true, the beautiful, the victorious way out of so much discouragement and so much crime,--that is the word "consecration." That word includes two essential ideas, the ideas of sacredness and cooperation. The problems of sex will never be solved until the sacredness of sex is recognized, for sex is vitally and indissolubly bound up with the two greatest facts that you and I know. The greatest fact of the organized world around us is life, the greatest fact of the spiritual world into which we lift our souls is love, and the beginnings of life and the beginnings of love are in sex. No boy or girl will readily understand what life means except as he has some clear, wise teaching about sex; no boy or girl will fully understand what love means except through recognition of the dignity and worth and purity of the fundamental facts and powers of sex.

Who shall give this enlightenment? I think it must be clear that this enlightenment cannot be given by the very young and inexperienced person, that the facts can be rightly given only by some person who knows their sacredness for himself or herself. They can be given best by a mature person who has seen and felt what they mean. In the long run, I have no doubt that our boys and girls will get the information that they must have from their parents, for the father and the mother are the best qualified to give it. I have named both the father and the mother, for the solution of our problem is not only in knowing the sacredness of sex, it is also in working together for the elevation of sex life. We shall not be able, we men, in the future, to sit down and say, "Oh, well, John will learn from his mother"; "Mary's mother will make that clear to her"; "Their mother does these things." It will not be possible for the socializing of the sex instincts and the ripening of the sex powers to be made clear to young people except as men and women both recognize the sacredness of the sex relation and undertake to make things clear to boys and girls. Men must give up their selfish indifference to evil conditions, and women--some women--must give up the bitterness and hardness that come into their hearts and their faces when they think of the suffering that their sex has endured at the hands of man. This is not a problem for one sex. It cannot be solved by either half of the great whole of humanity. We know this to be true in our personal life; it is equally true in our social life. It is only by the girding-up of the whole spirit of man to go forth and meet his duty as a lover, as a husband, as a father, and it is only by the girding-up of all the powers of the woman to lead and to help, that the family is organized. In this great human family of ours the man and the woman in days that are coming will cooperate to remove from our midst the blackest and most fearful perversion of the natural powers of our race. We do not believe in sitting down idly before this problem and saying, "It has always been, it always will be." In this great day of moral and spiritual progress, with powers that we have inherited from our forefathers in this land and other lands, we know that there is no necessary evil. We are learning what the evil of sex is, and how it arises, and we are beginning to use the forces at hand for its destruction. Conscience is kindling and determination is hardening among our people that this thing shall cease to be. The ape and the tiger shall yet die from our midst, and man's spirit shall triumph in his flesh.

Notes:

[59] A. Forel, ***The Sexual Question***, chap. XII, "Religion and Sexual Life"; William James, ***Varieties of Religious Experience***, chap. I; especially the first footnote.

[60] F.W. Foerster, ***Marriage and the Sex Problem***, chap. IV; especially section (d), "The Educational Significance of Monogamy."

CHAPTER XII

AGENCIES, METHODS, MATERIALS, AND IDEALS

By William Trufant Foster

At the outset we observed that the present social emergency is not concerned merely with diseases, or physiology, or laws, or wages, or suffrage, or recreation, or education, or religion. All of these phases of the present situation, and many others, must be taken into account in our attempted solution of the problem of sex hygiene and morals. A person who believes that he can offer a quick and certain way out of our difficulties appears to have no comprehension of the problem. This much, however, is certain: the greatest need is public education. The policy of silence has failed. Accurate and widespread knowledge is a necessary condition of progress, whatever may be the chosen direction. The main questions at issue concern the Agencies, Methods, Materials, and Ideals of education.[61] The following propositions are intended as a brief summary of the most important truths concerning each of those four aspects.

I. AGENCIES

1. As there are but few parents who can and will give the necessary instruction, it must be given by other agencies, at least until a new generation of parents has been prepared to meet this responsibility.

2. Although the failure of parents calls for the immediate action of other

agencies, the instruction should be so conducted as to break down the barriers of false modesty and establish confidence between parents and children.[62]

3. As the public school is the only agency of formal education that reaches nearly all of the children of the nation, sex instruction must eventually be given in all public schools; only thus can we bring forward a new generation of parents, equipped with the knowledge and desire to do their duty by their children.

4. As a majority of our boys and girls do not enter high school, some instruction in matters of sex should be given in grammar schools.

5. No community should introduce direct sex education into the schools as a part of the curriculum, until it has informed parents, cultivated favorable public opinion, and obtained the services of teachers who are qualified for the work by nature and by special preparation.

6. All normal schools and all college departments of education should at once embody, in their courses for teachers, instruction in the matter and methods of sex education, and adequate instruction should be provided for teachers now in service; and within a reasonable time after such opportunities have been offered in a given State, certificates to teach in that State should be granted only to those who have had the prescribed preparation.

7. As there is not now a sufficient number of public school teachers prepared to teach sex hygiene, such teaching must be done in part, at least for many years, by private agencies.

8. Lectures should be arranged for parents by churches, schools, colleges, clubs, granges, boards of health, and other organizations; but no one should be accepted as a lecturer until he is approved by a board of

health, social hygiene society, college, or other organization which is unquestionably competent to pass judgment on the qualifications of the speaker.

9. Since there are adults in every community that will not be reached, even when sex education becomes a part of the day-school curriculum, such instruction should be offered in continuation schools, in social settlements, in Young Men's Christian Associations, in college extension courses, in factories, stores, lumber-camps, car-shops,--indeed, wherever the happy connection can be made between those who need the help and those who are surely qualified to give help.[63]

II. METHODS

1. Sex instruction as a rule should not be isolated; it should not be prominent; it should be an integral part of courses in biology, hygiene, and ethics. "Specialists" in sex education are undesirable as teachers of boys and girls, in or out of school.

2. As there is a discrepancy between the age of puberty and the age of marriage, due to artificial conditions of modern society, it is important that sex consciousness and sex curiosity should develop slowly: accordingly, sex instruction, unlike instruction in other subjects, must seek to satisfy rather than to stimulate interest in the subject; questions must be answered truthfully, but the answers must not lead the curiosity of the child beyond the information that is immediately necessary for the guidance of his own conduct.

3. The aims of sex education can be fully attained only by the encouragement of every means for keeping the mind occupied throughout waking hours with wholesome thoughts and the body sufficiently active in vigorous work and play, preferably out of doors.

4. Lectures and class instruction should be provided only for carefully selected groups: almost nothing can be gained, and much may be lost, by presenting the subject before miscellaneous audiences.

5. At every age, in every class, there are likely to be individuals who need certain instruction not needed by the entire class: such instruction should be given privately.

6. Books dealing directly with human sex life should not be given to children before the age of puberty; some of the books most widely used are dangerous; instruction should come directly from parent or teacher.

7. Traveling exhibits, made up of concrete and vivid materials, and prepared with due consideration of all the accepted principles of sex education, may be used effectively and inexpensively to bring the truths before many thousands of adults in many places.[64]

8. Against commercialized prostitution, the educational campaign should be one of pitiless publicity: the public should know the names of all persons engaged in promoting the business, whether they are prostitutes (including female and male), or liquor dealers, owners of houses, owners of real estate, lessees, proprietors, financial backers, policemen, or politicians; their connection with the traffic should be proclaimed by means as effective as the "tin-plate" signs for disorderly houses.

9. Reliable investigations should be made further to reveal the relationships between sexual immorality and venereal diseases, on the one hand, and, on the other hand, between sexual immorality and ignorance, low wages, injurious clothing, lack of wholesome amusements, low dance-halls, grills, moving-picture houses, vaudeville shows and so-called legitimate theaters, mental deficiency, armies and navies, and--most important of all--the liquor traffic; and the outcome of such investigations should be

made known through persistent campaigns of public education.

10. The conclusions of every vice commission and of every other dependable investigation--not the details--must be kept before the public, until the truth is common knowledge that segregation never segregates; that safeguarding clinics never safeguard; that medical control never controls; that official protection of immorality increases immorality; and that, if there be any such thing as a necessary evil, it is not the shameless partnership of government and vice.[65]

III. MATERIALS

1. Elementary nature-study for children and biological study for boys and girls of high-school age may lead gradually and safely to the teaching of plant and animal reproduction, provided that the subject is not left on the plane of animal life; it is a mistake to suppose that the teaching of biology necessarily promotes right conduct in matters of sex.

2. Subordinate and incidental to instruction in normal sex processes, warning should be given of the dangers of individual vice, illicit sexual intercourse, and venereal diseases; but such instruction should be given only to groups that are homogeneous in respect to sex, physiological age, and social environment, or preferably, to individuals.[66]

3. Instruction concerning venereal disease, which leaves the impression that the chief danger of illicit intercourse is "getting caught," should not be tolerated: knowledge of facts though scientifically accurate, is not necessarily protection to the individual or to society.

4. As sex instruction for young people has none but practical aims, hygienic and moral, only such knowledge concerning sex processes, reproduction, and diseases should be given at each period as is necessary

for the welfare of the individual at that period.

5. The practice of masturbation is sufficiently common among both boys and girls to call for warnings to all children at the earliest ages; any teacher or parent should be qualified to help in individual cases.

6. The education of adolescent boys must stress the six great truths that will fortify them against the main arguments of the enemies of decency and health:--

(1) Sexual intercourse is not a physiological necessity; continence was never known to impair physical or mental vigor.

(2) There can be but one standard of chastity; the purity a man demands for his sister, he must achieve for himself.

(3) Seminal emissions are natural among healthy men; usually they need cause no concern.

(4) Gonorrhea is a terrible disease, with tragic consequences that one can never fully foretell; syphilis is worse.

(5) Every woman who offers her body for prostitution is, sooner or later, a probable source of contagion; clean living is the only positive safeguard against venereal disease.

(6) Nearly every "advertising specialist" is a criminal of the most contemptible type; the only safe adviser is the doctor in reputable standing who is not afraid to sign his name to his prescription or to his advice.

IV. IDEALS

1. "The function of education is to guide the intellect into a knowledge of right and wrong, to supply motives for right conduct, and to furnish occasions by which alone can moral habits be cultivated." (Drummond.)

2. The first aim of sex education is necessarily to bring about an open-minded, serious, if possible a reverent, attitude toward sex and motherhood, in place of the traditional secrecy and vulgarity; a teacher who cannot do this should do nothing.[67]

3. In so far as the sex life of animals is made the basis of instruction, the *difference* between man and the lower animals is the point to emphasize; otherwise the facts of animal life may appear to justify irresponsible sex activities, whereas the glory of man is his control over animal instincts.

4. Since it is not ignorance of what is right, but rather the will to do the right, that is usually responsible for sexual delinquency among adults, the program of public education must include more effective moral education in all grades of all schools; every subject, properly taught, is a means of cultivating will power, of strengthening character; but the school curriculum is now made to yield but a small part of its possibilities.

5. The appeal must be made to self-respect and to chivalry; especially through history and literature the idea of sex must be spiritualized; the right education of the emotions is fundamental.[68]

6. Through the study of heredity and eugenics, the social responsibility of the individual may be made to serve as a higher incentive for right conduct than the fear of disease.

7. If there is one truth concerning sex education that needs emphasis above all others, it is that all plans for meeting the social emergency must strengthen the control of moral and spiritual law over sex impulses; otherwise sex education may be antagonistic not only to physical health, but as well to the highest development of personality and to the progressive evolution of human society.

Notes:

[61] The best expression of the consensus of opinion of those who should know most about the subject is the ***Report of the Special Committee on the Matter and Methods of Sex Education*** issued by the American Federation for Sex Hygiene, New York, December, 1912.

[62] ***Sex Education***, by Ira S. Wile, M.S., M.D. (New York, 1912), aims to assist parents to banish the difficulties and to suggest a course of instruction. It is a brief and wholly admirable treatise.

[63] ***Progress***, the second annual report of the Oregon Social Hygiene Society, gives some account of the most extensive public education that has been conducted in this country.

[64] The Exhibit of the Oregon Social Hygiene Society has been seen by over 50,000 people, at a total cost of less than two cents for each person.

[65] Especially valuable are the two volumes by Abraham Flexner, written for the Bureau of Social Hygiene. See List of References.

[66] See ***American Youth***, New York, April, 1913 ("Sex Education Number"). An article by George W. Hinckley tells of the ideal way in which he gives individual instruction to his boys at Good Will Farm, Hinckley, Maine.

[67] "Sex-instruction as a Phase of Social Education," in *Religious Education*, 1913, by Maurice A. Bigelow, is one of the best articles on this subject.

[68] F.W. Foerster, *Marriage and the Sex Problem.* No book on this subject has reached a higher plane of idealism. At the same time it is scientifically sound.

LIST OF REFERENCES

CHAPTERS I, II

GENERAL SURVEY

Prepared by Maida Rossiter, Librarian, Reed College

Addams, Jane. *A New Conscience and an Ancient Evil.* New York, 1912.

American Federation for Sex Hygiene. Report of the Sex Education Sessions of the Fourth International Congress on School Hygiene. New York, 1913.

American Medical Association. ***Nostrums and Quackery.*** Chicago.

Bloch, Iwan. ***Sexual Life of our Time in its Relation to Modern Civilization***; tr. by Eden Paul. St. Louis, 1911.

Brieux, Eugene. ***Damaged Goods.*** In his ***Three Plays.*** New York, 1911.

Commonwealth Club of California. ***The Red Plague.*** Commonwealth Club of California. ***Transactions***, vol. VI, no. 1, May, 1911; vol. VIII, no. 7, August, 1913.

Dealey, J.Q. ***The Family in its Sociological Aspects.*** Boston, 1912.

Ellis, Havelock. ***Task of Social Hygiene.*** Boston, 1912.

Flexner, A. ***Prostitution in Western Europe.*** New York, 1913. Bureau of Social Hygiene Publications.

---- ***Prostitution in the United States.*** (In preparation.) Bureau of Social Hygiene Publications.

Foerster, F.W. ***Marriage and the Sex Problem***; tr. by Meyrick Booth. New York, 1912.

Forel, August. ***Sexual Question***; tr. by C.F. Marshall. New York, 1908.

Fosdick, R.D. ***European Police Systems.*** New York 1913.

Kneeland, G.J. ***Commercialized Prostitution in New York City.*** New York, 1913. Bureau of Social Hygiene Publications.

Morrow, P.A. ***Social Diseases and Marriage.*** New York 1904.

Northcote, Hugh. ***Christianity and Sex Problems.*** Philadelphia, 1906.

Seligman, E.R.A., ed. ***Social Evil.*** Ed. 2, rev. New York, 1912.

Sisson, E.O. ***Educational Emergency.*** Atlantic Monthly, vol. 106, pp. 54-63, July, 1910.

Thomson, J.A., ***and*** Geddes, P. ***Problem of Sex.*** New York, 1912.

Westermarck, Edward. ***History of Human Marriage.*** New York, 1903.

Wilson, R.N. ***American Boy and the Social Evil.*** Philadelphia, 1905.

Zenner, Philip. ***Education in Sexual Physiology and Hygiene.*** Cincinnati, 1910.

CHAPTER III

PHYSIOLOGICAL ASPECTS

Reproduction

Exner, M.J. *The Physician's Answer.* New York, 1913.

Howell, W.H. *Textbook of Physiology.* Ed. 4. Philadelphia, 1911.

Landois, Leonard. *Textbook of Human Physiology.* Ed. 10. Philadelphia, 1904.

Marshall, F.H.A. *Physiology of Reproduction.* New York, 1910.

Heredity and Eugenics

Castle, W.E. *Heredity.* New York, 1911.

Darbishire, A.D. *Breeding and the Mendelian Theory.* New York, 1911.

Davenport, C.B. *Heredity in Relation to Eugenics.* New York, 1911.

Ellis, Havelock. *Problem of Race Regeneration.* New York, 1911.

Jordan, D.S. *Heredity of Richard Roe.* Boston, 1911.

Kellicott, W.E. *Social Direction of Human Evolution.* New York, 1911.

Punnett, R.C. *Mendelism.* New York, 1911.

Saleeby, C.W. *Methods of Race Regeneration.* New York, 1912.

---- *Parenthood and Race Culture.* New York, 1909.

Walter, H.E. *Genetics.* New York, 1913.

Winship, A.E. *Jukes-Edwards; a Study in Education and Heredity.*
Harrisburg, 1900.

CHAPTER IV

MEDICAL PHASES

Dock, L.L. *Hygiene and Morality; Medical, Social and Legal Aspects of
Venereal Diseases.* New York, 1910.

Fisher, Irving. *National Vitality.* Washington, 1910. U.S. 61st Cong., 2d
Sess. Senate Doc. 419.

Hall, W.S. *Biology, Physiology, and Sociology of Reproduction* also, *Sexual Hygiene.* Ed. 11. Chicago, 1906.

Keyes, E.L. *Observations of the Persistence of Gonococci in the Male Urethra.* American Journal of the Medical Science, January, 1912.

Morrow, P.A. *Social Diseases and Marriage.* Philadelphia, 1904.

Taylor, R.W. *Practical Treatise on Genito-Urinary and Venereal Diseases and Syphilis.* Ed. 3. Philadelphia, 1904.

CHAPTER V

ECONOMIC PHASES

Adams, T.S., *and* Sumner, H.L. *Labor Problems.* Ed. 8. New York, 1911. Chap. I.

Addams, Jane. *A New Conscience and an Ancient Evil.* New York, 1912.

Butler, E.B. *Women and the Trades.* New York, 1909.

Flexner, Abraham. *Prostitution in the United States.* New York. (In preparation.) Bureau of Social Hygiene Publications.

---- ***Prostitution in Western Europe.*** New York, 1913. Bureau of Social Hygiene Publications.

Fosdick, R.D. ***European Police Systems.*** New York, 1913. Bureau of Social Hygiene Publications.

Goldmark, Josephine. ***Fatigue and Efficiency.*** New York, 1912.

Kelley, Florence. ***Some Ethical Gains through Legislation.*** New York, 1905.

Kneeland, G.J. ***Commercialized Prostitution in New York City.*** New York, 1913. Bureau of Social Hygiene Publications.

More, L.B. ***Life Earner's Budgets; A Study of Standards and Cost of Living in New York City.*** New York, 1907.

Roe, C.G. ***Panders and their White Slaves.*** Chicago, 1910.

Ryan, J.A. ***A Living Wage.*** New York, 1910.

Sanger, W.W. ***History of Prostitution.*** New York, 1913.

Seligman, E.R.A., ed. ***Social Evil.*** Ed. 2, rev. New York, 1912. Chap. I.

Streightoff, F.H. ***Standard of Living among Industrial People of America.*** Boston, 1911.

U.S. Bureau of Labor. ***Women and Child Wage-Earners in the United States.*** Washington, 1911-12. Vols. 5, 15.

U.S. Immigration Commission. ***Steerage Conditions; Importation and Harboring Women for Immoral Purposes....*** Washington, 1911. U.S. 61st Cong., 3d Sess. Senate Doc. 753.

Reports of Commission, vol. 37.

Vice Commission Reports.

A list of vice commissions is printed at the end of these references.

CHAPTER VI

RECREATIONAL PHASES

Addams, Jane. ***Spirit of Youth and the City Streets.*** New York, 1912.

Allen, W.H. ***Civics and Health.*** Boston, 1909.

Camp-Fire Girls of America. ***Manual.*** New York, 1913.

Chicago Vice Commission. ***Report***, 1911.

Collier, John. ***Moving Pictures; Their Function and Proper Regulation.*** Playground Magazine, vol. 4, pp. 232-39, October, 1910.

Health Department Control of Venereal Diseases. Social Diseases, vol. 2, nos. 2-3, April and July, 1911.

Israels, Mrs. C.H. *Dance Problem.* Playground Magazine, vol. 4, pp. 242-50, October, 1910.

Juvenile Protective Association of Chicago. Reports on dance halls, moving picture theaters, saloons, department stores, etc. Chicago, 1911-12.

Minneapolis Vice Commission. *Report*, 1911, pp. 129-31.

Perry, C.A. *Wider Use of the School Plant.* New York, 1910.

Playground Association of America. *Proceedings*, 1907 to date. New York, 1908 to date.

Russell Sage Foundation. Recreation Bibliography. New York, 1912.

Ward, E.J., ed. *Social Centers.* New York, 1913.

CHAPTER VII

EDUCATIONAL PHASES

American Federation for Sex Hygiene. *Proceedings*, 1913. New York, 1913. Report of the Sex Education Sessions of the Fourth International Congress on School Hygiene and the Annual Meeting of the Federation at Buffalo,

August 27-29, 1913.

---- Report of Special Committee on the Matter and Methods of Sex Education. Presented before the Sub-Section on Sex Hygiene of the Fifteenth International Congress on Hygiene and Demography, held in Washington, D.C., September 23-28, 1912. New York City, 1913.

Cocks, O.G. ***Engagement and Marriage: Talks with Young Men.*** New York, 1913. Sex Education Series. Study no. 4.

Cook, W.A. ***Problems of Sex Education.*** Journal of Educational Psychology, vol. 4, pp. 253-60, May, 1913.

Ellis, Havelock. ***Studies in the Psychology of Sex.*** Philadelphia, 1900-10. 6 vols.

Hall, G.S. ***Adolescence.*** New York, 1908. Chap. VI.

---- ***Educational Problems.*** New York, 1911. Chap. VII.

Hall, W.S. ***Sexual Knowledge.*** Philadelphia, 1913.

---- ***Strength of Ten.*** 1909.

Henderson, C.R. ***Education with Reference to Sex.*** National Society for the Scientific Study of Education. 8th Yearbook, 1909.

Lyttleton, Edward. ***Training of the Young in Laws of Sex.*** New York, 1900.

Manny, F.A. Bibliography of Sex Hygiene. ***Educational Review***, vol. 46, pp. 168-76, September, 1913.

Moll, Albert. *Sexual Life of the Child.* New York, 1912.

Phelps, Jessie. *Teaching of Sex in Normal Schools.* National Conference of Charities and Corrections. *Proceedings*, 1912, pp. 267-70.

Putnam, H.C. *Sex Instruction in Schools.* National Society for the Scientific Study of Education. 8th Yearbook, 1909, pt. 2.

Society of Sanitary and Moral Prophylaxis. Educational pamphlets.
   No. 1. *Young Man's Problem.*
   No. 2. *Instruction in Physiology and Hygiene of Sex for Teachers.*
   No. 3. *Relations of Social Diseases with Marriage and their Prophylaxis.*
   No. 4. *Boy Problem.*
   No. 5. *How my Uncle the Doctor instructed me in Matters of Sex.*
   No. 6. *Health and Hygiene of Sex.*

Thomas, W.I. *Sex and Society.* Chicago, 1907.

Wagner, Charles. *Youth.* New York, 1905. Book 3.

Warthin, A.S. *Sex Pedagogy in the High School.* In Johnston, C.H., ed., High School Education. New York, 1912.

Wile, I.S. *Sex Education.* New York, 1912. Bibliography, pp. 149-50.

Willson, R.N. *American Boy and the Social Evil.* Philadelphia, 1905.

---- *Education of the Young in Sex Hygiene; A Textbook for Parents and Teachers.* Philadelphia, 1913.

CHAPTER VIII

TEACHING PHASES

For Children

Chapman, Mrs. Rose Wood Allen. ***How Shall I Tell my Child?*** Chicago, 1912.

Hall, W.S. ***Strength of Ten.*** 1909.

Lyttleton, Edward. ***Training of the Young in Laws of Sex.*** New York, 1900.

Moll, Albert. ***Sexual Life of the Child.*** New York, 1912.

Morley, Margaret. ***Renewal of Life.*** Chicago, 1906.

Torelle, Ellen. ***Plant and Animal Children; how they grow.*** Boston, 1912.

CHAPTER IX

TEACHING PHASES

For Boys

Boys' Venereal Peril. Chicago, 1911. (16-18 years.)

Hall, W.S. *From Youth into Manhood.* New York, 1910. (11-15 years.)

---- *Instead of Wild Oats.* Chicago, 1912.

---- *John's Vacation; A Story for Boys.* Chicago, 1913.

---- *Life's Beginnings.* New York, 1912. (10-14 yrs.)

Lowry, E.B. *Truths; Talks with a Boy concerning himself.* Chicago, 1911.

Morley, M.W. *A Song of Life.* Chicago, 1902. (Young men.)

Oker-Blom, Max. *How my Uncle, the Doctor, instructed me in Matters of Sex.* Society of Sanitary and Moral Prophylaxis. Educational Pamphlet no. 5. (10-14 years.)

Sperry, L.B. *Confidential Talks with Young Men.*

Wegener, Hans. *We Young Men.* Philadelphia, 1911. (21 years and upward.)

Wilson, R.N. *American Boy and the Social Evil.* Philadelphia, 1905. (18 years and upward.)

---- *Nobility of Boyhood.* Philadelphia, 1910. (14-18 years.)

Young Man's Problem. New York, 1912. Society of Sanitary and Moral Prophylaxis. Educational Pamphlet no. 1.

CHAPTER X

TEACHING PHASES

For Girls

Chamberlain, A.F. *The Child; A Study in the Evolution of Man.* Ed. 2. London, 1911.

Cleaves, M.A. *Education in Sexual Hygiene for Young Working Women.* Charities and the Commons, vol. 15, pp. 721-24, Feb. 24, 1906.

Dudley, Gertrude, *and* Kellor, F.A. *Athletic Games in the Education of Women.* New York, 1909.

Gesell, A.L. *Normal Child and Principles of Education.* Boston, 1912.

Goldmark, J.C. *Fatigue and Efficiency.* New York, 1912.

Gordon, H.L. *Modern Mother.* New York, 1909.

Hall, W.S. *The Doctor's Daughter; A Story for Girls.* Chicago, 1913.

---- *Life Problems; A Story for Girls.* Chicago, 1913.

Johnson, G.E. *Education by Plays and Games.* Boston, 1907.

Lowry, E.B. *Herself; Talks with Women concerning themselves.* Chicago, 1911.

---- *False Modesty.* Chicago, 1912.

---- *Confidences; Talks with a Young Girl concerning herself.* Chicago, 1910.

Mosher, E.M. *Health and Happiness.* New York, 1912.

Oppenheim, Nathan. *Care of the Child in Health.*

---- *Development of the Child.* New York, 1908.

Partridge, G.E. *Genetic Philosophy of Education.* New York, 1912.

Plain Talks with Girls about their Health and Physical Development. Salem, 1912. Oregon State Board of Health. Circular no. 4.

Puffer, J.A. *The Boy and his Gang.* Boston, 1912.

Saleeby, C.W. *Woman and Womanhood.* New York, 1911.

Smith, N.M. *Three Gifts of Life.* New York, 1913.

Sperry, L.B. *Confidential Talks with Young Women.* Chicago, n.d.

Tyler, J.M. *Growth and Education.* Boston, 1905.

CHAPTER XI

MORAL AND RELIGIOUS PHASES

Abbott, Lyman. *Womanhood.* Oregon Social Hygiene Society. Circular no. 16.

Bible. Mark X, 2-12. Compare Deut. XXIV, 1-4.

Bible. Matt. V, 27-30.

Bible. I Cor. 7.

Foerster, F.W. *Marriage and the Sex Problem.* New York, 1912.

Hall, G.S. *Adolescence.* New York, 1908. Chaps. XIII-XV.

Hamilton, Cosmo. *A Plea for the Younger Generation.* New York, 1913.

James, William. *Varieties of Religious Experience.* New York, 1911. Chap. I.

PERIODICALS

The following periodicals are sources of news in regard to sex education, sex hygiene, and allied subjects:--

American Breeders' Magazine; A Journal of Genetics and Eugenics. Published quarterly by the American Breeders' Association. Washington, D.C. Sent to members, annual membership, $2.00.

American Medical Association: *Journal.* Published weekly by the American Medical Association, 535 Dearborn Avenue, Chicago, Ill. $5.00 yearly.

American Physical Education Review. Published monthly by the American Physical Education Association, Springfield, Mass. $3.00 yearly.

Eugenics Review. Published quarterly by the Eugenics Education Society, 6, York Buildings, Adelphi, London. *4s. 6d.* yearly.

Journal of Educational Psychology. Published monthly, except July and August, by Warwick & York, Baltimore, Md. $2.50 yearly.

Social Diseases. Published quarterly. 105 West 40th Street, New York City. $1.00 yearly.

Survey; A Journal of Constructive Philanthropy. Published weekly by the Survey Associates, 105 East 22d Street, New York City. $2.00 yearly.

Vigilance. A monthly magazine correlating constructive efforts for the suppression of the social evil. Published monthly by the American Vigilance Association, 156 Fifth Avenue, New York City. $1.00 yearly.

U.S. Commissioner of Education. Monthly record of current educational publications. Bibliography, published monthly, devotes one section to sex hygiene. Sent free from Commissioner's Office, Washington, D.C.

ORGANIZATIONS INTERESTED IN SOCIAL HYGIENE

American Federation for Sex Hygiene. Combined with American Vigilance Association to form American Social Hygiene Association.

American Health Defense League. 37 Liberty Street, New York City.

American Medical Association. 535 Dearborn Avenue, Chicago. Secy., Dr. Alex. R. Craig.

American Purity Alliance. 207 East 15th Street, New York City.

American Social Hygiene Association. 105 West 40th Street, New York City. Secys., Dr. William Snow, J.B. Reynolds.

American Unitarian Association. Department of Social and Public Service. Committee on Sex Education and Hygiene. Boston, Mass.

American Vigilance Association. Combined with American Federation for Sex Hygiene to form American Social Hygiene Association.

Bureau of Social Hygiene. Members: Davis, Katharine B.; Warburg, Paul M.;

Murphy, Starr J.; Rockefeller, John D., Jr., Chairman. P.O. Box 579, New York City.

California Social Hygiene Society. San Francisco. Secy., C.N. White.

Chicago Society of Social Hygiene. 100 State Street, Chicago. Secy., W.T. Belfield.

Colorado Society for Social Health. Denver, Colo.

Committee of Fourteen. 27 E. 22d Street, New York City. Secy., F.H. Whitin.

Commonwealth Club of California. 804 First National Bank Building, San Francisco, Cal.

Connecticut Society of Social Hygiene. 42 High Street, Hartford, Conn. Secy., T.N. Hepburn.

Detroit Society for Sex Hygiene. 33 High Street E., Detroit, Mich. Secy., Raymond E. Van Syckle.

Friends' Committee on Philanthropic Labor. Park Avenue and Laurens Street, Baltimore, Md.

Illinois Vigilance Association. 153 Lasalle Street, Chicago.

Indiana Society of Social Hygiene. 723 Hume-Mansur Building, Indianapolis, Ind. Secy., Dr. H.G. Hamer.

Indiana State Board of Health. Indianapolis, Ind. International Congress on School Hygiene. Fourth meeting held in Buffalo, August 27-29, 1913.

International Purity Association.

Juvenile Protective Association. 816 South Halsted Street, Chicago.

Los Angeles Society of Social Hygiene. 311 Higgins Building, Los Angeles, Cal.

Maryland Society of Social Hygiene. 15 E. Pleasant Street, Baltimore, Md. Secy., Howard C. Hill.

Massachusetts Association of Boards of Health. Boston, Mass.

Massachusetts Society for Sex Education. 7 Hancock Avenue, Boston, Mass.

Massachusetts State Board of Health. State House, Boston, Mass.

Mexican Society of Sanitary and Moral Prophylaxis of Venereal Diseases.

Milwaukee Society of Social and Moral Hygiene. Milwaukee, Wis.

National Conference of Charities and Corrections. Angola, Ind. Secy., Alexander Johnson.

National Consumers' League. 105 East 22d Street, New York City.

National Education Association. Ann Arbor, Mich. Secy., D.W. Springer.

National Purity Association. 79 Fifth Avenue, Chicago.

New Jersey Society for the Prevention of Social Diseases. East Orange, N.J. Secy., Dr. Thomas N. Gray.

New York State Reformatory for Women at Bedford. Laboratory of Social

Hygiene. Supt., Katharine Bement Davis.

New Zealand Society of Sanitary and Moral Prophylaxis.

Oregon Social Hygiene Society. 703 Selling Building, Portland, Ore. Secy., H.H. Moore.

Oregon State Board of Health. 720 Selling Building, Portland, Ore. Secy., Dr. Calvin S. White.

Pacific Coast Federation for Sex Hygiene. Portland, Ore. Secy., H.H. Moore.

Pennsylvania Society for the Study and Prevention of Social Diseases. 1708 Locust Street, Philadelphia. Secy., R.N. Wilson.

Rhode Island State Board of Health. State House, Providence, R.I.

St. Louis Society of Social Hygiene. St. Louis, Mo. Secy., Dr. H.E. Kleinschmidt.

School of Eugenics of Boston. 168 Newbury Street, Boston, Mass.

Seattle Society of Hygiene. League Building, Seattle, Wash. Secy., Dr. Sydney Strong.

Social Purity and White Cross Movement. The Philanthropist, P.O. Box 2554, New York City.

Society of Sanitary and Moral Prophylaxis. 611 Tilden Building, 105 West 40th Street, New York City. Secy., Dr. E.L. Keyes, Jr.

Spokane Society of Social and Moral Hygiene. 420 Old National Bank

Building, Spokane, Wash. Secy., Dr. J.R. Lantz.

Texas State Society of Social Hygiene. San Antonio, Texas. Secy., Dr. T.Y. Hull.

Triennial Congress for the Suppression of the White Slave Traffic. Fifth meeting held in London, June 30-July 4, 1913.

Washington State Board of Education. Olympia, Washington.

West Virginia Society of Social Hygiene. Elkins, West Va. Secy., O.G. Wilson, Supt. of Public Schools.

World's Purity Federation. LaCrosse, Wis. Pres., B.S. Steadwell.

REPORTS AND INVESTIGATIONS

MUNICIPAL

Atlanta, Ga. Vice Commission. ***Report***, 1912.

Chicago. Vice Commission. ***Social Evil in Chicago.*** Chicago, 1911.

Cleveland. Vice Commission. ***Report***, 1911.

Columbia, Mo. Vice Commission. Appointed March, 1913.

Columbus, Ohio. Appointed March, 1913.

Denver, Colo. Vice Commission. Appointed September 15, 1912. Became Denver Morals Commission January 31, 1913.

Grand Rapids. Morals Efficiency Commission of the Citizens. To carry on work started by Committee of 41.

Hartford, Conn. Vice Commission. Appointed January, 1912.

Jacksonville, Fla. Vice Commission. Appointed September, 1912.

Kansas City. Vice Commission. *Report*, 1912.

Little Rock, Ark. Vice Commission. *Report*, 1912.

Macon, Ga. Vice Commission. Appointed January, 1913.

Minneapolis. Vice Commission. *Report*, 1911.

New York City--
  Seligman, E.R.A., ed. *Social Evil.* New York, 1912.
  Kneeland, G.J. *Commercialized Prostitution in New York City.* New York, 1913.

Philadelphia. Vice Commission. *Report.* Philadelphia, 1913.

Portland, Ore. Vice Commission. *Report*, 1913.

Rochester. Vice Commission. *Report.*

St. Paul, Minn. Morals Committee. *Report.*

San Francisco--

Commonwealth Club of California. ***Report on Prevalence of Venereal Diseases.*** February, 1911.

Shreveport, La. Vice Commission. Appointed April, 1913.

Syracuse. Moral Survey Committee. ***Report on the Social Evil in Syracuse.*** 1913.

STATE

Illinois. Vice Commission. Appointed February, 1913.

Maryland. Vice Commission. Appointed March, 1913.

Massachusetts. Vice Commission. Established April, 1913.

Missouri. Vice Commission. Appointed April, 1913.

Wisconsin. Vice Commission. Established May, 1913.

STANDING COMMISSIONS

Pittsburg, Pa. Morals Efficiency Commission. Appointed May, 1912. Chairman, Frederick A. Rhodes.

Minneapolis. Morals Commission. Appointed March, 1913. Chairman, Dr.

Marion D. Shutter.

Denver. Morals Commission. Appointed January 31, 1913. Chairman, Rev. H.F. Rail.

New York. Committee of Fourteen.

Chicago. Morals Court.

The Codes Of Hammurabi And Moses
W. W. Davies

The discovery of the Hammurabi Code is one of the greatest achievements of archaeology, and is of paramount interest, not only to the student of the Bible, but also to all those interested in ancient history...

Religion   **ISBN:** *1-59462-338-4*

QTY

Pages:132
MSRP $12.95

The Theory of Moral Sentiments
Adam Smith

This work from 1749. contains original theories of conscience amd moral judgment and it is the foundation for systemof morals.

Philosophy   **ISBN:** *1-59462-777-0*

QTY

Pages:536
MSRP $19.95

Jessica's First Prayer
Hesba Stretton

In a screened and secluded corner of one of the many railway-bridges which span the streets of London there could be seen a few years ago, from five o'clock every morning until half past eight, a tidily set-out coffee-stall, consisting of a trestle and board, upon which stood two large tin cans, with a small fire of charcoal burning under each so as to keep the coffee boiling during the early hours of the morning when the work-people were thronging into the city on their way to their daily toil...

Childrens   **ISBN:** *1-59462-373-2*

QTY

Pages:84
MSRP $9.95

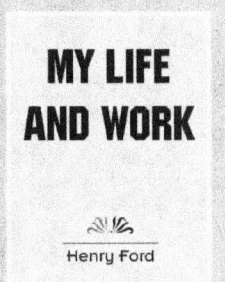

My Life and Work
Henry Ford

Henry Ford revolutionized the world with his implementation of mass production for the Model T automobile. Gain valuable business insight into his life and work with his own auto-biography... "We have only started on our development of our country we have not as yet, with all our talk of wonderful progress, done more than scratch the surface. The progress has been wonderful enough but..."

Biographies/   **ISBN:** *1-59462-198-5*

QTY

Pages:300
MSRP $21.95

The Art of Cross-Examination
Francis Wellman

QTY

I presume it is the experience of every author, after his first book is published upon an important subject, to be almost overwhelmed with a wealth of ideas and illustrations which could readily have been included in his book, and which to his own mind, at least, seem to make a second edition inevitable. Such certainly was the case with me; and when the first edition had reached its sixth impression in five months, I rejoiced to learn that it seemed to my publishers that the book had met with a sufficiently favorable reception to justify a second and considerably enlarged edition. ..

Pages:412

Reference   ISBN: *1-59462-647-2*   *MSRP $19.95*

On the Duty of Civil Disobedience
Henry David Thoreau

QTY

Thoreau wrote his famous essay, On the Duty of Civil Disobedience, as a protest against an unjust but popular war and the immoral but popular institution of slave-owning. He did more than write—he declined to pay his taxes, and was hauled off to gaol in consequence. Who can say how much this refusal of his hastened the end of the war and of slavery ?

Law   ISBN: *1-59462-747-9*   **Pages:48**

MSRP $7.45

Dream Psychology Psychoanalysis for Beginners
Sigmund Freud

QTY

Sigmund Freud, born Sigismund Schlomo Freud (May 6, 1856 - September 23, 1939), was a Jewish-Austrian neurologist and psychiatrist who co-founded the psychoanalytic school of psychology. Freud is best known for his theories of the unconscious mind, especially involving the mechanism of repression; his redefinition of sexual desire as mobile and directed towards a wide variety of objects; and his therapeutic techniques, especially his understanding of transference in the therapeutic relationship and the presumed value of dreams as sources of insight into unconscious desires.

Pages:196

Psychology   ISBN: *1-59462-905-6*   *MSRP $15.45*

The Miracle of Right Thought
Orison Swett Marden

QTY

Believe with all of your heart that you will do what you were made to do. When the mind has once formed the habit of holding cheerful, happy, prosperous pictures, it will not be easy to form the opposite habit. It does not matter how improbable or how far away this realization may see, or how dark the prospects may be, if we visualize them as best we can, as vividly as possible, hold tenaciously to them and vigorously struggle to attain them, they will gradually become actualized, realized in the life. But a desire, a longing without endeavor, a yearning abandoned or held indifferently will vanish without realization.

Pages:360

Self Help   ISBN: *1-59462-644-8*   *MSRP $25.45*

QTY

The Rosicrucian Cosmo-Conception Mystic Christianity *by Max Heindel* ISBN: *1-59462-188-8* **$38.95**
The Rosicrucian Cosmo-conception is not dogmatic, neither does it appeal to any other authority than the reason of the student. It is: not controversial, but is: sent forth in the, hope that it may help to clear... *New Age/Religion Pages 646*

Abandonment To Divine Providence *by Jean-Pierre de Caussade* ISBN: *1-59462-228-0* **$25.95**
"The Rev. Jean Pierre de Caussade was one of the most remarkable spiritual writers of the Society of Jesus in France in the 18th Century. His death took place at Toulouse in 1751. His works have gone through many editions and have been republished... *Inspirational/Religion Pages 400*

Mental Chemistry *by Charles Haanel* ISBN: *1-59462-192-6* **$23.95**
Mental Chemistry allows the change of material conditions by combining and appropriately utilizing the power of the mind. Much like applied chemistry creates something new and unique out of careful combinations of chemicals the mastery of mental chemistry... *New Age Pages 354*

The Letters of Robert Browning and Elizabeth Barret Barrett 1845-1846 vol II ISBN: *1-59462-193-4* **$35.95**
by Robert Browning and Elizabeth Barrett *Biographies Pages 596*

Gleanings In Genesis (volume I) *by Arthur W. Pink* ISBN: *1-59462-130-6* **$27.45**
Appropriately has Genesis been termed "the seed plot of the Bible" for in it we have, in germ form, almost all of the great doctrines which are afterwards fully developed in the books of Scripture which follow... *Religion/Inspirational Pages 420*

The Master Key *by L. W. de Laurence* ISBN: *1-59462-001-6* **$30.95**
In no branch of human knowledge has there been a more lively increase of the spirit of research during the past few years than in the study of Psychology, Concentration and Mental Discipline. The requests for authentic lessons in Thought Control, Mental Discipline and... *New Age/Business Pages 422*

The Lesser Key Of Solomon Goetia *by L. W. de Laurence* ISBN: *1-59462-092-X* **$9.95**
This translation of the first book of the "Lernegton" which is now for the first time made accessible to students of Talismanic Magic was done, after careful collation and edition, from numerous Ancient Manuscripts in Hebrew, Latin, and French... *New Age/Occult Pages 92*

Rubaiyat Of Omar Khayyam *by Edward Fitzgerald* ISBN:*1-59462-332-5* **$13.95**
Edward Fitzgerald, whom the world has already learned, in spite of his own efforts to remain within the shadow of anonymity, to look upon as one of the rarest poets of the century, was born at Bredfield, in Suffolk, on the 31st of March, 1809. He was the third son of John Purcell... *Music Pages 172*

Ancient Law *by Henry Maine* ISBN: *1-59462-128-4* **$29.95**
The chief object of the following pages is to indicate some of the earliest ideas of mankind, as they are reflected in Ancient Law, and to point out the relation of those ideas to modern thought. *Religiom/History Pages 452*

Far-Away Stories *by William J. Locke* ISBN: *1-59462-129-2* **$19.45**
"Good wine needs no bush, but a collection of mixed vintages does. And this book is just such a collection. Some of the stories I do not want to remain buried for ever in the museum files of dead magazine-numbers an author's not unpardonable vanity..." *Fiction Pages 272*

Life of David Crockett *by David Crockett* ISBN: *1-59462-250-7* **$27.45**
"Colonel David Crockett was one of the most remarkable men of the times in which he lived. Born in humble life, but gifted with a strong will, an indomitable courage, and unremitting perseverance... *Biographies/New Age Pages 424*

Lip-Reading *by Edward Nitchie* ISBN: *1-59462-206-X* **$25.95**
Edward B. Nitchie, founder of the New York School for the Hard of Hearing, now the Nitchie School of Lip-Reading, Inc, wrote "LIP-READING Principles and Practice". The development and perfecting of this meritorious work on lip-reading was an undertaking... *How-to Pages 400*

A Handbook of Suggestive Therapeutics, Applied Hypnotism, Psychic Science ISBN: *1-59462-214-0* **$24.95**
by Henry Munro *Health/New Age/Health/Self-help Pages 376*

A Doll's House: and Two Other Plays *by Henrik Ibsen* ISBN: *1-59462-112-8* **$19.95**
Henrik Ibsen created this classic when in revolutionary 1848 Rome. Introducing some striking concepts in playwriting for the realist genre, this play has been studied the world over. *Fiction/Classics/Plays 308*

The Light of Asia *by sir Edwin Arnold* ISBN: *1-59462-204-3* **$13.95**
In this poetic masterpiece, Edwin Arnold describes the life and teachings of Buddha. The man who was to become known as Buddha to the world was born as Prince Gautama of India but he rejected the worldly riches and abandoned the reigns of power when... *Religion/History/Biographies Pages 170*

The Complete Works of Guy de Maupassant *by Guy de Maupassant* ISBN: *1-59462-157-8* **$16.95**
"For days and days, nights and nights, I had dreamed of that first kiss which was to consecrate our engagement, and I knew not on what spot I should put my lips..." *Fiction/Classics Pages 240*

The Art of Cross-Examination *by Francis L. Wellman* ISBN: *1-59462-309-0* **$26.95**
Written by a renowned trial lawyer, Wellman imparts his experience and uses case studies to explain how to use psychology to extract desired information through questioning. *How-to/Science/Reference Pages 408*

Answered or Unanswered? *by Louisa Vaughan* ISBN: *1-59462-248-5* **$10.95**
Miracles of Faith in China *Religion Pages 112*

The Edinburgh Lectures on Mental Science (1909) *by Thomas* ISBN: *1-59462-008-3* **$11.95**
This book contains the substance of a course of lectures recently given by the writer in the Queen Street Hail, Edinburgh. Its purpose is to indicate the Natural Principles governing the relation between Mental Action and Material Conditions... *New Age/Psychology Pages 148*

Ayesha *by H. Rider Haggard* ISBN: *1-59462-301-5* **$24.95**
Verily and indeed it is the unexpected that happens! Probably if there was one person upon the earth from whom the Editor of this, and of a certain previous history, did not expect to hear again... *Classics Pages 380*

Ayala's Angel *by Anthony Trollope* ISBN: *1-59462-352-X* **$29.95**
The two girls were both pretty, but Lucy who was twenty-one who supposed to be simple and comparatively unattractive, whereas Ayala was credited, as her Bombwhar romantic name might show, with poetic charm and a taste for romance. Ayala when her father died was nineteen... *Fiction Pages 484*

The American Commonwealth *by James Bryce* ISBN: *1-59462-286-8* **$34.45**
An interpretation of American democratic political theory. It examines political mechanics and society from the perspective of Scotsman James Bryce *Politics Pages 572*

Stories of the Pilgrims *by Margaret P. Pumphrey* ISBN: *1-59462-116-0* **$17.95**
This book explores pilgrims religious oppression in England as well as their escape to Holland and eventual crossing to America on the Mayflower, and their early days in New England... *History Pages 268*

QTY

The Fasting Cure by *Sinclair Upton*   ISBN: *1-59462-222-1*   **$13.95**

In the Cosmopolitan Magazine for May, 1910, and in the Contemporary Review (London) for April, 1910, I published an article dealing with my experiences in fasting. I have written a great many magazine articles, but never one which attracted so much attention... New Age/Self Help/Health Pages 164

Hebrew Astrology by *Sepharial*   ISBN: *1-59462-308-2*   **$13.45**

In these days of advanced thinking it is a matter of common observation that we have left many of the old landmarks behind and that we are now pressing forward to greater heights and to a wider horizon than that which represented the mind-content of our progenitors... Astrology Pages 144

Thought Vibration or The Law of Attraction in the Thought World   ISBN: *1-59462-127-6*   **$12.95**

by *William Walker Atkinson*   *Psychology/Religion Pages 144*

Optimism by *Helen Keller*   ISBN: *1-59462-108-X*   **$15.95**

Helen Keller was blind, deaf, and mute since 19 months old, yet famously learned how to overcome these handicaps, communicate with the world, and spread her lectures promoting optimism. An inspiring read for everyone... Biographies/Inspirational Pages 84

Sara Crewe by *Frances Burnett*   ISBN: *1-59462-360-0*   **$9.45**

In the first place, Miss Minchin lived in London. Her home was a large, dull, tall one, in a large, dull square, where all the houses were alike, and all the sparrows were alike, and where all the door-knockers made the same heavy sound... Childrens/Classic Pages 88

The Autobiography of Benjamin Franklin by *Benjamin Franklin*   ISBN: *1-59462-135-7*   **$24.95**

The Autobiography of Benjamin Franklin has probably been more extensively read than any other American historical work, and no other book of its kind has had such ups and downs of fortune. Franklin lived for many years in England, where he was agent... Biographies/History Pages 332

Name	
Email	
Telephone	
Address	
City, State ZIP	

☐ **Credit Card**   ☐ **Check / Money Order**

Credit Card Number	
Expiration Date	
Signature	

Please Mail to: Book Jungle
PO Box 2226
Champaign, IL 61825
or Fax to: 630-214-0564

ORDERING INFORMATION

web: *www.bookjungle.com*
email: *sales@bookjungle.com*
fax: *630-214-0564*
mail: *Book Jungle PO Box 2226 Champaign, IL 61825*
or PayPal *to sales@bookjungle.com*

Please contact us for bulk discounts

DIRECT-ORDER TERMS

20% Discount if You Order
Two or More Books
Free Domestic Shipping!
Accepted: Master Card, Visa,
Discover, American Express

www.ingramcontent.com/pod-product-compliance
Lightning Source LLC
Chambersburg PA
CBHW080823020726
47501CB00009B/2391